Love in the Age of Dinosaurs

Sorcha Lang

This is a work of fiction. Names, characters, places and events described herein are products of the author's imagination or are used fictitiously and are not to be construed as real. Any resemblance to actual events, locations, organizations, or persons, living or dead, is entirely coincidental.
Love in the Age of Dinosaurs
Copyright © 2012 by
Elizabeth F. Hill and Nalini K. Unny
Front cover design
Copyright © 2012 by Judith B. Glad
Also published electronically by
Uncial Press,
http://www.uncialpress.com

All rights reserved. Except for use in review, the reproduction or utilization of this work in whole or in part in any form by any electronic, mechanical or other means now known or hereafter invented, is forbidden without the written permission of the publisher.

Copyright © 2012 Sorcha Lang
All rights reserved.

ISBN: 1-4783-9824-8
ISBN-13: 9781478398240

Dedication

For our families

The authors first heard the 'one-finger oath' on an amazing tour at Dinosaur Provincial Park. We also wish to thank the technicians at the Royal Tyrrell Museum in Drumheller who so patiently and thoroughly answered our many questions.

This novel would not have reached publication without the support and encouragement of our readers: Margaret Allen, Rita Marler, Patricia Olafson, Anne O'Regan, Vicky Reed, Jane Schmidt, Rhonda Serink, Elizabeth Sheppard, Lilian Simmonds, Heather Stock, Theresa Tether, Latha Unny, Noreen Westel. Our thanks and our love.

Lastly, we wish to thank our editor, Judith B. Glad, from whom we have learned so much.

~~~

"Just what the devil do you think you're doing?"

Startled, Sara jumped back, twisted her foot on a rock and started to tumble.

He caught her tightly by the left arm and hauled her to her feet.

"Oh! I-I-I was just—"

"Trespassing?" The man did not loosen his hold.

As Sara attempted to break free, she glared up into eyes the colour of cornflowers. "Do you mind? You're hurting my arm."

He glared back. "You've no business here. This part of the park is a World Heritage site, and is off-limits for under-dressed, overly-curious little teen-agers who think they can traipse around anywhere they please, regardless of regulations." He marched her over to a sign that read STRICTLY OFF-LIMITS. AUTHORISED PERSONNEL ONLY.

Sara stared, speechless. But just as she opened her mouth with a tart retort, Patrick appeared around a rock outcropping.

"Well." He beamed. "I see you two have already met. Sara, this is Thomas McBride, the head of our research team. Tom, you're manhandling the amazing Sara Wickham, your competition for Palaeontologist of the Modern Era and the woman whom I've been telling you so much about."

chapter

ONE

It's not an easy thing, Sara reflected, *to fire an assistant.* She thought about Kelly—how hard she worked, her eagerness to please, her willingness to work overtime on the shortest of notice—and she wondered how she could possibly fire Kelly. *So how should one fire a good assistant? Is it best to start hinting a few weeks in advance so that she knows what's coming? Do you start finding fault with the work that's being done, so that she knows what's coming? Or do you do what Andrew has just done to me?*

"Sara, are you listening to me?" said Andrew Turner, the director of the museum and her immediate supervisor.

"I think you might have lost me for a minute there, right after that bit about how you're firing me because I'm so competent."

Andrew leaned back in his chair. "You're not being fired. At least, not permanently. Think of it as strongly encouraged temporary leave. Once you finish that funding application, you are free to take a compulsory three-month vacation. With my blessing, of course."

A compulsory three-month vacation was not, in Sara's view, the appropriate reward for all of her hard work and her excellent relationships with her colleagues. All of her colleagues minus one. She narrowed her eyes as she began to wonder if Andrew had been unduly influenced by that one negative voice.

"Does this have anything to do with that last field report that Adrian filed?" she said suspiciously. "There were some serious gaps in that malicious little missive, you know."

"Gaps in Adrian's report?" Andrew repeated in a tone of disbelief. "I can't say that I noticed any in Adrian's report. But I did notice a few tiny omissions in yours and Jay's. Little things like failure to observe proper safety precautions, harebrained risk-taking, serious physical injuries, to name a few."

"I thought I explained." Sara sighed.

"You did. You explained everything at great length. I think it was the most elegant explanation I have ever received from anyone: organised, detailed, informative, intelligent, interesting. And obviously a fabrication. You didn't really expect me to believe it, did you?"

Sara opened her mouth to interrupt, but Andrew continued.

"You are the most talented young palaeontologist I have on staff. You excel at every aspect of palaeontology. You work harder than any palaeontologist I have ever known. Since you joined us, we have received more funding and made more stunning fossil discoveries than ever before. Every single one of your colleagues—except Adrian, of course—loves working with you, and I have here several international requests from other palaeontologists eager to collaborate with you." He gestured at a pile of papers on his desk. "The Australians want you back for fieldwork this summer, as do the Chinese and the South Americans."

"But—"

"But," Andrew said, "this is the summer that you are going to forego fieldwork, office work, and any other work and go on vacation."

"But Andrew, I don't want to go on vacation. I don't need to go on vacation. Vacations are for people who like vacations. I don't like vacations."

Andrew leaned forward and grasped her chin, forcing her to meet his eyes. "You need a break, Sara. It's been at least three years, probably longer, since you've taken even a day off work. You're driving yourself too hard. You're exhausted and it's starting to affect your judgement in the field. You need some time off before you have another serious accident."

"It was only a broken wrist," Sara said. "I need—"

"Some time off," Andrew said, and his words sounded final. "Three months off, starting tomorrow. I do not want you to join any expeditions; nor do I want you studying, discovering, writing, or thinking about dinosaurs for the next three months. At the end of three months, if I am satisfied that you are sufficiently rested, you will be reinstated. And if I am not satisfied with your course of conduct, I can assure you that you will be even less satisfied with mine."

Sara gazed at him in consternation. She noted, as she always did, how good-looking he was. Tall, fair, blue-eyed, and young. Only five years older than herself, an amazing palaeontologist in his own right, a wonderful boss, and generally very easy to get along with. Perhaps she could appeal to his easy-going nature. "Okay, how about if I take the next month off and then join one of the teams—"

Andrew slapped his palm on the desktop. "Sara. We are not bargaining. We are setting a new precedent. I am the boss. You are my subordinate. This is one time that you will do as I say and I say that you will take three months off."

She shrank back into her chair and gaped at him. He had never spoken to her like this before. Far from being a micromanager, he usually gave her a wide scope to make her own decisions about her own work and any work that he passed along to her.

Occasionally, he'd called her on the carpet for neglecting safety precautions in the field, and occasionally he lectured her about working too hard, but all in all, they'd had an excellent working relationship. She had generally felt quite comfortable ignoring him. "I can't believe you are doing this. For heaven's sake, this is the twenty-first century. Where are your priorities? You should be working me to death, not forcing me to take time off."

"I don't have to work you to death," Andrew said. "You're doing a fine job of that yourself. My priority is to protect my assets for the long term. I want you working for me for a long time to come. So in the short term, you need some time off. Starting tomorrow." He stood and came around the desk.

Sara just looked at him and threw up her hands.

Andrew pulled her to her feet. "C'mon, Sara." He gave her a hug. "This interview is over. You're fired. Now go and have a great summer."

Sara arrived in her assistant's office with no recollection of how she had gotten there. She went on into her own office and quickly walked back out again. "Kelly?"

"Uh huh?" Kelly didn't look up from an article she was reading.

"Where's my computer?"

"Your computer?" Kelly looked up blankly.

"You know. Silver laptop. Mirror image of yours. Usually sits on my desk. Useful for research, e-mails, word-processing."

"Oh. That computer." Kelly looked like she was trying not to laugh. "It's gone."

"I know it's gone. Did it say where it was going and when it is coming back?"

The attempt failed, and Kelly grinned. "I believe it had a date. With Andrew. At least, he's the one who picked it up and took it away. Not seeing any other machines at the moment, is he?"

Sara blew out her breath in exasperation. "Did Andrew say what he expects me to do without a computer? I still have work to do today, which, in case you don't know, is my last day."

"I heard rumours that you were going to be taking some time off. A vacation. Do you remember what that is, Sara?"

Sara sank down onto a chair in front of Kelly's desk. "Yeah. Forced retirement for the near future. What're you reading?"

"An article by Thomas McBride on a newly discovered *Pachyrhinosaurus lakustai* in northern Alberta. He's just gorgeous."

"Yeah, isn't he? I love the bosses on his nose."

"Not the *Pachyrhinosaurus*. Thomas McBride. Not only famous and brilliant, but also an indisputable ten." Kelly rotated the journal so that Sara could see the author's photograph.

Sara considered it for a moment. "Oh, I don't know. He's all right, I guess. If you like wavy black hair and perfect features. But a ten? It all depends on how tall he is and what colour his eyes are. A ten requires six feet and blue eyes. And a nice smile. He looks kind of serious."

Kelly's laughter filled the small office. "Are you kidding? He's drop-dead gorgeous. No debate. Maybe he looks serious in the picture because it's a serious article. Maybe he's serious about his work, like others I could name. Oh, speaking of serious..."

She rifled through some papers on her desk and handed Sara a memo. "Here. Patrick O'Regan called while you were closeted with Andrew. He said it was very important that you call him back today."

"Patrick? Of course, I'll call right now."

"Well, maybe you should read his e-mail first. Andrew had me transfer all of your e-mails onto my computer so that you could deal with them before you left. And I have the funding application, too. You just need to check it over and take a hard copy. Then I guess you're done for the day. Or rather, for the month. Or rather, for the next three months." She stood and stepped out of the way.

Sara sat down and scrolled through her e-mails. There weren't many, because she had dealt with most of them before lunch. She had been on her way back when Andrew had requested that she step into his office for a few minutes. Having no idea of the bombshell he was about to drop on her, she had been happy to comply.

Love in the Age of Dinosaurs

Sara was still having a hard time believing that she was going to be spending the next three months on a compulsory vacation.

She responded to the work-related messages before opening Patrick's e-mail. She raised her eyebrows as she read. She scrolled back up and clicked on the attachments, which she printed. Then she printed off the e-mail as well and headed into her office, where she hunched over her desk with her fingers kneading her forehead, and re-read Patrick's e-mail.

> So Mary is off work for the duration of the pregnancy. We've also lost four other team members due to illness or injury. That, plus the horrible weather we've had this year, has resulted in a dismal field season. It's half over and we haven't accomplished a quarter of what we had set out to do. Thomas is really under the gun, trying to do the regular field work and trying to find the resources to devote to the park boundary issue.
>
> You've never met Thomas, but I know you'd like him. His reputation as one of the world's foremost palaeontologists is well deserved, and he's a heck of a nice guy besides. And the team he's put together is just great. And that's why I'm asking for your help. It's been a long, long time since you've been back to Alberta, and I know that you're not keen to return—and I don't blame you—but we do desperately need your help. I'm sending some photos of our camp at Dinosaur Provincial Park and I've marked in your spot. All I ask is that you give it some serious thought. I'll call you.
>
> Love, Patrick

Sara studied the photos she had printed off. She rearranged them to make a composite picture of the camp. There was one main road going into Dinosaur Provincial Park. At the park entrance, it branched. To the left, it wound through to the public campground. To the right it led to a parking area across from the palaeontologists' field station, a plain grey stone building with a lean-to on one end. *Probably a tool shed.*

There was one Jeep in the photo, but it looked like the parking area was big enough for a few more vehicles. A path from the field station meandered through some trees to a campground, where a large picnic shelter stood next to a huge fireplace and a couple of picnic tables. Nearby was an enormous tent, and from what she could see, it held tables and chairs.

Sara squinted. It looked like there was a work area with burners or camp stoves inside the shelter. In the centre of the camping area was a sizeable fire pit with benches all around. A dozen or so domed tents were pitched along the line of the stream. Patrick had drawn an arrow to one of the domes and had labelled it "Sara's tent".

Sara was reaching for the phone when it rang.

She held the receiver to her ear and heard the familiar voice of her old friend. "Wow, Sara. What's happening to you? I didn't even know that you ever took lunch breaks, let alone a two-and-a-half-hour one. Or do you just save up and take one long one once a month?"

"Ha. Ha," Sara said. "Very funny."

"It would be if I weren't talking about you," Patrick replied. "Have you been taking proper care of yourself? You looked like a rake when I saw you a few weeks ago."

Sara rolled her eyes. "I'm fine, how's Mary?"

"Very tired. The doctor thinks she's doing too much. Mary says that if she becomes any less active than she is now, people will assume she is dead and send her to a mortuary instead of a maternity wing."

Sara chuckled. "Well, Mary has never been a great one for inactivity. I'm sure it's frustrating for her. I wish I could see her."

"Why don't I book you a flight? You did tell her—"

"And I meant it," Sara said. "I promise I'll be there, Patrick. If not before, then definitely right after, the birth. Even though I hate Alberta, I promise to be there."

"Well, since you promise to come, why not make it sooner than later? Did you get my e-mail?"

"Yes. Just a few minutes ago, as a matter of fact."

"Well...Are you interested?"

"Of course I'm interested. You knew I would be. And I'm flattered that you've invited me. In fact, I was just about to call you back."

"To say it's an offer you can't refuse and you're on your way."

"No, sorry. I'd like to help—you must know that—but it's out of the question."

"Why?" Patrick practically barked the word.

"You know very well why."

"No, actually I don't. What's the excuse this time?"

Sara's tone became as testy as Patrick's. "Two reasons. One, I'm not planning to return to Alberta—"

"Sara, don't you think it's too soon..."

"No, Patrick, it certainly is not too soon to make that decision. I've been thinking about it for five long years. I am never moving back to Alberta. Besides, I'm starting a summer holiday."

She yanked the phone away from her ear. "You know, Patrick, it's very rude to make those kinds of noises on the telephone."

Patrick started to talk again and Sara cautiously moved the phone closer. As she listened, her annoyance faded and she began to feel very guilty. Patrick had never sounded so desperate.

"Please, Sara," he was saying. "We all need you this summer. Mary, Thomas, and I. If Thomas can't turn things around soon, the whole programme will go down the tubes. And if there was ever a time that Mary and I needed you, it's now. You don't have to stay the whole summer. Six weeks will see us through."

Sara felt her resolve weakening. She was tempted. So tempted. How could she fail her friends in their time of need? And a chance to work with Thomas McBride! So young, and already a legend in the field. But why oh why did he have to work in Alberta?

She gripped the phone more tightly as she strained to catch Patrick's words. He was speaking very softly, almost as if he were talking to himself. "Okay, Sara, I guess you're not ready. Forget I asked. Go and have your holiday."

Sara felt something crack inside. She could take Patrick's scorn. She was impervious to his anger. But sadness? That was unexpected and it cut her to the quick. The words spurted out. "Okay, fine, whatever, have it your way, but six weeks only, not one minute longer."

"You're aware that you'll need Andrew's clearance?"

"Of course."

"Okay, I'll get on it right away. Since it's your vacation time, there shouldn't be any problem. It's basically just a formality."

"No don't!" Sara hoped she hadn't sounded as panic-stricken as she felt. She struggled to speak more calmly. "You do not need to contact him. I will do all of the necessary informing."

"You sure? You sound a little stressed. Thomas or I can easily do it."

"I'm only coming if you promise me that you are not going to call Andrew. I'll talk to you tonight about the reservations. 'Bye, Patrick."

Thoughtfully, Sara hung up the phone and covered her face with her hands. *I think I just heard myself agreeing to go back to Alberta, which is the very last place on earth I want to be. How did Patrick do that?* Her stomach began to churn. *Why, why, why did I agree?*

"Don't tell me, Sara!" Kelly sounded annoyed. "Don't tell me that you are not leaving on vacation this evening. Don't tell me that you are once again putting your own well-being on hold to do a favour for a friend. Don't tell me that some dinosaur somewhere that's been waiting sixty-five million years to be dug up and catalogued *cannot* wait until after your holiday to make your acquaintance."

Sara said, "I did try to say no. But I can't. He's too good a friend and we go back too far. We were friends in high school, roomed together through undergrad, spent our graduate years doing research together. I actually introduced him to his wife, Mary. They were bricks when…Well, anyway. I can't just walk away when Patrick needs my help."

"And that is what makes you Sara," Kelly said, with a wry smile. "We wouldn't have you any other way. But please tell me that he only needs your help for a day or two."

"Well, actually, it might just be a teensy bit longer than that. Guess who he's collaborating with out in Dinosaur Provincial Park—Thomas McBride!"

"They've had serious setbacks in their field season this year. Weather, equipment, staffing—you name it. I don't have all the details yet, but Patrick says they really need my assistance for a few weeks—six at most."

"Six weeks? That's half your holiday time. I've a good mind to go straight to Andrew and tell him what you're doing."

Sara immediately recognised that no argument in the world was going to persuade Kelly to turn a blind eye while she went off to do summer field work for six weeks. Kelly truly looked like she had every intention of reporting to Andrew. So, Sara jettisoned her arguments and salvaged the situation with her weapon of last resort. "Please, Kelly?"

Kelly seemed to be trying to see inside Sara's head as looked into her eyes for several minutes. Finally she said, "Fine. Six weeks. Not a day longer. If, in six weeks, I don't get an e-mail from some ocean paradise describing in detail all those great six-packs on the beach, I'm going straight to Dr. Turner and letting him know what you're up to. And you know he said that if terminating your employment was the only way to get you to slow down, by God, he'd do it."

Sara blinked. "How do you know he said that? I haven't had a chance to tell you yet."

"He practised on me first," Kelly admitted. "He said that this was one time you weren't going to talk him out of his decision. He really means it. And so do I."

"Okay, Kelly." Sara clasped Kelly's hands in her own. "It's a deal. You promise not to say a word to anyone about where I am and what I'm doing. I will wrap everything up in six weeks and head for the hills." Kelly frowned and she amended, "I mean the beach."

"What Dr. Turner doesn't know, will prevent him from getting apoplexy. So a little secrecy is all in his best interest, wouldn't you say?"

Kelly gave Sara a brief, tight hug and quickly left the office.

chapter

TWO

Sara gripped the door handle tightly as the truck jounced over a rut in the road and sent her flying upwards toward the roof. Luckily, this time she didn't make contact. She had already banged her head twice and she was beginning to think it would be a minor miracle if she actually made it into the park without a serious concussion.

"Sorry about that." The farmer glanced over at her. "The road's been in terrible shape all summer. It's been washed out several times from all the storms we've been having. Poured again this morning as you can see by the puddles. We've had more rain this year than in the last ten altogether. And *The Farmers'*

Sorcha Lang

Almanac is predicting a lot more precipitation before we're done this year."

"Oh, that's okay, Ben" Sara replied lightly. "People are always telling me I need some sense knocked into me." She couldn't remember now why she had ever agreed to come to Dinosaur Provincial Park. The trip had been a total nightmare so far. Her red-eye flight had encountered severe turbulence, causing several people to be sick, including the child who had managed to throw up all over Sara's seat. Then, when thick fog and lightning had prevented the plane from landing in Calgary, the plane had been re-routed to Lethbridge.

The phone lines had been jammed for hours, and when she'd finally made contact with the research station, she was only able to talk to the camp cook, whose speech was a rich southern gumbo spiced with words like "dis", "dat", and "d'otha". His Creole accent was so strong that she'd found herself pressing the phone painfully into her ear, as if that would help her to distinguish the unfamiliar Cajun sounds. She had absolutely no idea what "yat" meant, so she'd just explained where she was and what she planned to do, eliciting a merry "Well, if dat don' put peppa in da gumbo," in response.

She was pretty sure she would have remembered it if Patrick had mentioned that their camp cook was from the back bayous of Louisiana. She wondered what the rest of the team were like. It didn't look as if she was about to meet them anytime soon.

She'd ended up taking a local bus to Taber, but the highway north to Brooks was closed for construction. She'd had to thumb rides from local farmers. She'd ridden high in a tractor pulling a load of hay, had squeezed between straw bales in the back of a half-ton pickup, and now was holding on for dear life in the cab of this dilapidated pickup. Rusty springs stuck out of the worn and torn leather seat. She was pretty sure that the truck had made its appearance before they invented suspension systems for vehicles.

"Nearly there," Ben announced as they rounded a curve in the road. "Just to your right, there, in that field, you can see the prehistoric tipi rings. They say the Indians never camped in the Badlands, just set themselves up on the prairie rim surrounding it. It was something like a holy place for them."

The truck began a steep winding descent into the Park. Sara felt goosebumps rise on her arms at the sight of the innocuous eternal prairie spiralling down into the exposed sandstone moonscape of the Badlands. Striated layers of golden and rust-coloured sandstone contrasted warmly with the clear azure sky, the deepest blue on the continent. Distant hoodoos appeared like sentries wearing jaunty tams guarding hidden treasure.

Although some of that treasure had already been discovered and shared out amongst the world's museums, there were untold caches of dinosaur treasure still to be unearthed. As always, Sara felt awed and humbled to be a part of the excavation of the earth's history.

She leaned closer to the windshield, surrendering herself to the familiar pull of the landscape. Yet even as she marvelled that she had forsaken this place for so long, her gorge rose. A potent surge of nausea thrust her back against the seat, and she wondered in despair how she could bear to stay.

"You okay, Sara?" Ben frowned with apparent concern. "You look a little green about the gills."

With a supreme effort, Sara swallowed the bile that she was gagging on and surreptitiously wiped her cold clammy hands on her jeans. "Oh, I'm fine, thanks. Just a little tired, that's all."

"Good thing it's just another minute." Ben applied the brakes as they entered the parking area.

"Thank you so much, Ben," Sara said, as she gingerly made her way to the ground from the high cab seat when the pickup rolled to a stop. She still wasn't too sure that nothing was broken after the jolting ride.

"No problem. Glad to be of help. Hey, Barney." He bent to pet a lively-looking red cocker spaniel who looked enormously pleased to meet them. "Hi, there, Dave. How's it goin'? Hear your team loves your cookin'."

Sara turned to see a tall, pleasant-looking youth who was grinning from ear to ear. As he hopped back into the cab, Ben said, "Sara, this is Dave, camp cook. Sara's the new member of your team." He spun his truck in a quick U-turn and headed back down the lane with a spurt of gravel.

Dave stuck out his hand and, his eyes twinkling, said, in a soft, educated Canadian accent, "Pleased to meet you, Sara. You're not exactly what I pictured when I spoke to you on the phone."

Sara goggled, and began to laugh and said, "Likewise, I'm sure. And are you the real camp cook?"

"Sorry about that. I have an audition with the Rosebud Theatre at the end of the summer and I like to practise my improv for an hour a day. The phones are out and the crew is all in the field, so there's been no one to talk to. When you called, it seemed like too good an opportunity to pass up." He laughed as he picked up Sara's bag. "Just so you know, you handled it really well. Much better than Thomas the night I was rehearsing a scene where I had to alert the troops that a fire was consuming the camp." His laughter was unrepentant. "I have to keep

Love in the Age of Dinosaurs

reminding Tom that if I could provoke a reaction like that, it means I was really, really convincing."

"And how did Thomas respond?" Sara couldn't help being amused.

"We-ell, them thar's words that shore ain't fit fer a lady's ears," Dave replied with a Texan drawl. "Or mine either." He switched off the accent. "They're still ringing. Y'know, it takes a lot to rile the guy, but the end result is sure worth the effort." He grinned cheerfully.

Sara found herself smiling back.

"I'll show you to your quarters, madam." Dave used an upper class British accent this time. "This way, please." He glanced behind. "C'mon, Barney. Let's go."

The dog wagged his tail and trotted up beside them. Dave indicated Barney and said, "Tom's dog. He's the camp mascot. Friendly to everyone, but reserves his love for Tom. Follows him everywhere. When Tom's not around, Barney parks himself in the shade of Tom's tent and waits for him. He'll come and accept food from the rest of us, but we've never seen him leave the camp without Tom."

At the end of the lane, they turned towards the collection of tents that followed the line of the stream. Dave unzipped the screen of a compact two-person tent and deposited Sara's bag inside. "There you go. It's small, but you'll be able to stand up inside. You might want to rest or take a look around. The Jeep's over there. Keys are in the ignition.

"Let me know if you need anything. I'll be in the dining tent." Dave left, cheerfully whistling "Cabaret".

Sara sank onto the thick navy sleeping bag laid out on a fully inflated air bed. She stretched for a few minutes before jumping to her feet.

She had been longing for a chance to stretch out and sleep, sleep, sleep. But now that she was here, she was too keyed up to rest. Scores of submerged memories were bubbling so close to the surface that if she stayed a minute longer in her tent she'd be drowning in them. Even as she tarried to change her clothes, she fancied that the nylon sides were closing in on her. She would suffocate without some space and some fresh air. She just had to be out and a part of the amazing world that surrounded her.

She rummaged through her bag and pulled out a cotton tee-shirt, a pair of short shorts, and a beige Tilley hat. She changed quickly and thrust the hat over her wavy chestnut hair.

Apart from the hat, this wasn't her usual working uniform, but the temperature must have climbed to at least forty degrees centigrade. The hot sun felt good on her legs. She filled a water bottle at the pump, and bent down to pet Barney, who appeared out of nowhere, wagging his tail. The dog trotted beside her as she walked to the car, and then looked expectantly up at her as she climbed into the driver's seat.

"Want to come for a ride, Barney?" Sara invited. She laughed as Barney hopped in and settled himself in the passenger seat. Sara backed the Jeep out of its parking space and headed up the road signposted "Centrosaurus Bone Bed."

After fifteen minutes of driving, Sara reached the end of the road. She parked and consulted the map in the glove compartment. A ten-minute hike would probably get her to the bone bed.

Grabbing her water bottle, she started up the trail. She called Barney, but he looked at her curiously, tilted his head, and settled himself in the shade of a cottonwood tree.

Oh well, he'll be all right there for a short time. I shan't be too long.

Ten minutes later, with the bone bed not yet in sight, she was beginning to think that it might have been wiser to wait for the other team members to give her a guided tour. The terrain was much rougher than she had anticipated, the sun hotter, and she was pretty sure the rattlesnake slithering across the path up ahead was real, and not a mirage. She decided to keep going for another ten minutes, and then turn back if her goal was still not in sight.

Nine minutes later, she was rewarded with the sight of clear plastic sheets glinting in the sunlight. She must be looking at a metre box. Unable to resist taking a look, Sara crouched beside the cover and folded back the nearest corner. Sure enough, the plastic sheets were covering exposed bones that the team was in the process of extracting.

She inhaled sharply as she took in the number of bones and fragments strewn before her. She had known, of course, that there could be as many as sixty bones per square metre at this site, but somehow knowing that fact was not quite the same as actually seeing it with her own two eyes. Spellbound, she started to examine the find, and was soon wholly engrossed in identifying the uncovered fossils.

Considerable time had passed when she guiltily realised that she had stayed longer than planned. She looked regretfully at a right orbital horn, touched it softly with her finger.

"Just what the devil do you think you're doing?"

Startled, Sara jumped back, twisted her foot on a rock and started to tumble.

He caught her tightly by the left arm and hauled her to her feet.

"Oh! I-I-I was just—"

"Trespassing?" The man did not loosen his hold.

As Sara attempted to break free, she glared up into eyes the colour of cornflowers. "Do you mind? You're hurting my arm."

He glared back. "You've no business here. This part of the park is a World Heritage site, and is off-limits for under-dressed, overly-curious little teen-agers who think they can traipse around anywhere they please, regardless of regulations." He marched her over to a sign that read STRICTLY OFF-LIMITS. AUTHORISED PERSONNEL ONLY.

Sara stared, speechless. But just as she opened her mouth with a tart retort, Patrick appeared around a rock outcropping.

"Well." He beamed. "I see you two have already met. Sara, this is Thomas McBride, the head of our research team. Tom, you're manhandling the amazing Sara Wickham, your competition for Palaeontologist of the Modern Era and the woman whom I've been telling you so much about."

chapter

THREE

Sara felt the blood drain from her face. In the same instant, Thomas dropped her arm as if she had leprosy. In the ensuing silence, Patrick stepped forward to re-fasten the plastic sheets in position. "Well, I'm glad we've finally found you. I might've known you'd head straight into the research zone. We came across Barney by the Jeep and figured you had probably hiked up to examine the bone bed. Is there anything else you especially want to see before we head back?"

Before Sara could reply, Thomas said, "I think Miss Wickham has had quite enough sight-seeing for one day. She is getting quite a sunburn, and it really doesn't look as if she has sufficient water to be out much longer. Shall we?" He motioned her to precede him back down the trail.

Sara could feel warmth in her cheeks, warmth she knew was due less to the sun's rays, than to her embarrassment at having gotten off to such a disastrous start with one of the world's pre-eminent palaeontologists. *Not that I've done anything wrong! Really, the man is insufferable!*

The three of them walked back to the parking lot in silence, the only sounds the crunch of gravel under their feet. As they neared the cottonwoods, Barney came up to greet them. Thomas bent over to pet the dog. "It's not like Barney to hitch a ride with a stranger. And speaking of hitching, how did you happen to meet Ben Stowe? Dave said you arrived in his pickup."

A mild question, and a reasonable one. But she was hot, tired, embarrassed, and not at all in the mood for reasonable questions. Still smarting at the way Thomas had mistaken her for a teen-aged tourist and at the high-handed way he had terminated her little expedition, she decided it was none of his business how she had met Ben. "He drove me to the park and dropped me at the gate. He seemed to know Dave really well."

"Yes," said Thomas. "And how did you meet Ben Stowe?"

"I guess he's pretty well known around here." Sara shrugged. "He said his family has been farming the area for over a hundred years. He had such an interesting—"

"—way of avoiding the question. I'll ask you a third time, Sara. How is it that instead of informing me as to your whereabouts when your plane arrived in Lethbridge and waiting for my instructions, you turn up hours and hours later in the back of a rundown pickup driven by a local farmer?"

"You are sadly misinformed," Sara replied, shaking her head and giving him a look of pity. "I was certainly not in the back of that pickup."

Thomas raised an eyebrow.

"I rode in the cab with Ben, and while that is a step up from the back of the pickup, I must caution that it is definitely not the most luxurious of ways to travel. I do hope that in the future you will be able to make better arrangements for me."

Patrick snorted. "Aw, c'mon Sara, answer the question. How did you get from Lethbridge to Dinosaur Provincial Park?"

Sara chewed thoughtfully on her lower lip while she considered her answer. "Well, I used public transport, and then I met Ben and he offered me a ride."

"You can't get farther north than Taber on the bus," said Thomas. "Suppose you start explaining in detail how you got here from Taber."

Sara gave them a quick précis of her adventures since the airport.

"You're telling me that you took rides with three different strangers rather than wait in safety for a ride from the people who were expecting you."

"So what? They're all people well known around here."

"Well-known to us, yes, but not to you," Thomas pointed out.

"You know better than to hitchhike, Sara," Patrick said. "It isn't safe, even here."

"Well, what was I to do?" She'd had enough of the third degree. "It wasn't exactly my first choice, you know. I couldn't get hold of anyone, there wasn't a soul in the car rental place, and what passes for public transit wasn't exactly adequate or even available."

Patrick started to reply, but Thomas forestalled him.

"'Nuff said, Pat. I think we've made the point sufficiently. But just in case the point has not been fully taken," he said pleasantly, locking eyes with Sara, "don't ever let me catch you doing something like that again. Clear?"

"Crystal."

"Good." He turned to Patrick. "Sara can ride with you and I'll take the dog with me."

He turned on his heel and called Barney.

The dog, to Sara's intense satisfaction, turned his back on Thomas and hopped in with her as soon as she opened her door.

Thomas raised an eyebrow and began to laugh. Then, lifting his hand in a mock salute, got into his Jeep and drove away.

chapter

FOUR

"That insufferable man!" Sara fumed as Patrick manoeuvred the Jeep around a crater in the road. "He doesn't even know to be insulted when his loyal dog deserts him for a virtual stranger. Is he always like that?"

Patrick smiled. "Pretty much. He's an easy-going guy. He didn't like you in his bone bed, but who would? You know what you're doing, but a lot of amateurs end up messing about in restricted places. We've caught more than a few tourists pocketing bones to take home as souvenirs." He stole a glance at her. "It could have been a lot worse, you know. We've been chasing you down all day. First to Calgary, then to Lethbridge, then Taber, then here. He was quite worried about what might have happened to you. You were a bit flippant, you know."

Sara stretched out her legs. "So what happens now?"

Patrick replied, "Well, most of the crew will have returned. You should have time for a shower before we eat. It's just past eight now. At this time of year the sun doesn't fully set 'til about ten o'clock. We usually eat on benches around the fire pit and, weather permitting, have some music before bed. Besides Dave, whom you've met already, there are a few others who play musical instruments. It's a good group of people, so I think you'll be happy here."

As the Jeep came to a halt in the parking lot, Sara hopped out. Patrick came around the other side to give her a hug. "Haven't had a chance to properly say hello. And thanks for coming. It's great to have you here." Releasing her, he pointed. "The shower rooms are down there, just follow the signs. See you later." He strode off.

Sara entered her tent to collect her toiletries and a towel. She couldn't wait to stand under a stream of nice hot water and wash away the dirt and frustrations of the day.

An hour later she emerged from her tent dressed in slim black jeans and a soft linen shirt with a thin stripe of emerald that matched her eyes. She'd slung a sweater over her shoulders because the night had grown cool. That, she well knew, was always the case in Alberta, especially when the skies were clear. No matter how high the thermometer climbed during the day, it cooled off at night. When she went to bed, she would definitely need that warm sleeping bag that lay unfurled in her tent. She took a deep breath and caught the smell of the meat that Dave had barbecued for supper. She realised that she was famished.

Patrick strolled over. "There you are. Let's go over to the dining tent and I'll introduce you to the others. We'll be last in line, but don't worry, there's always plenty. Barbecued ribs and corn tonight. I don't know which comes first, the menu or the monologue, but usually the supper matches whichever role Dave has chosen to rehearse during the day. He's always changing character, but the food is always delicious."

They entered the screened enclosure and joined the other members of the team at the laden trestle table. Sara had never seen such a spread at a field station before. Luscious barbecued ribs, steaming corn on the cob, new potatoes roasted in their jackets, baked beans, and freshly made corn bread. Everything mouth-watering and piping hot. In the middle of the table there was a crisp green salad, and a quick glance down at the end revealed fresh fruit and chocolate chip cookies for dessert, as well as tea and coffee.

While she filled her plate, Patrick introduced her. "Alan, Barry, Samantha, and Mike are all graduate students doing field research. And there, trying to beat me to the ribs are Rob and Geoff and Laura, technicians from the museum. You and Tom have met, of course, and here's Dave, our local welcome wagon for stray palaeontologists."

Dave looked Sara over and nodded his head approvingly. "Well, Ma'am, you shore do clean up purdy." He grinned at Thomas. "Whaddaya say, Tom? Like her new look?"

Thomas gave Sara a teasing glance. "Shore do. I'd say you wear those freckles very well. Not that the mud splotches weren't attractive."

Sara put her hands on her hips, pretended to glare at Dave, and said, "You wretch! You might have pointed me in the direction of the showers rather than leaving me at large to frighten the countryside. Why didn't you tell me how I looked?"

Dave looked pained. "And deprive you of the opportunity to see for yourself the wonderful ways our bodies tell the tales of our travel choices? Besides, why give a woman a reason to break your arms when she will probably think of a hundred reasons to dismember you without your help?" He squeezed her shoulders gently and adopted a sincere tone. "Anyway, I personally thought you looked just fine. I assure you—cross my heart and hope to die—that I have absolutely no idea who started those rumours about a Gorgon arriving in mid-afternoon. I wouldn't have told you to have a look around if I hadn't been almost sure that anyone looking at you would not turn to stone." He jerked his thumb in Thomas's direction, "I trust you see what a prudent fellow I am and will put in a good word about me with the head honcho."

Sara burst into laughter. "You're impossible!"

"Well, the head honcho is going to want a word with you, David, regarding your telephone answering skills," Thomas said. "Book me some time in your busy social calendar."

Dave waved Thomas on. "Later, Tom, later. You know how I hate to mix pleasure with business."

Sara followed Patrick outside and seated herself beside him on a wooden bench. Seconds later, Barney appeared, wagged his tail hopefully, and put his head on her knee, managing to look as if he hadn't eaten in days. She gave him a piece of meat and he thumped his tail with pleasure. "Is Thomas annoyed with Dave?"

"Frequently." Patrick spread butter on his baked potato. "Dave is Tom's only cousin. He's a bit of a character, as I'm sure you've noticed. His father is a judge and Dave was actually quite a good student academically, but he decided he wanted to become

Love in the Age of Dinosaurs

an actor. His parents weren't too happy about it. They insisted that he had to get some training in something that would lead to a job and better security than acting. I think they had in mind something like medicine, but Dave insisted on culinary school. He graduated this spring, but couldn't find a job. So Thomas hired him as camp cook. I don't think Tom's expectations were too high, but Dave has certainly exceeded them, at least when it comes to cooking."

Thomas joined them in time to hear the last sentence. "Speaking of my wayward cousin? I heard about that telephone call you made while we were gone. David can get really carried away sometimes. It must have been quite bad today if even Dave realises he went too far. So, I do apologise for the rough beginning to your stay with us. Hopefully Dave's cooking will more than make up for the inadequacy of our welcome upon your arrival." He paused and smiled at Sara. "You and Dave seem to have hit it off."

"I think he's cute," she said. "He reminds me of..." She paused to watch as Thomas tossed a piece of meat to Barney, who leapt agilely into the air to catch it and swallowed it before he reached the ground again. "Wow! Did you see that? He's not exactly an advertisement for chewing your food thoroughly before taking the next bite, is he?"

"What or whom?"

Sara looked up from her plate. "What or whom what?"

"Dave reminds you of someone or something."

"Oh," Sara replied, deliberately vague. "Just of someone I used to know." She decided to change the subject. "So is this the complete team?"

"Yes," Thomas said. "Of course, every morning groups will arrive to help with the digs. Volunteers sign up for a three-week stretch, which gives us time to train them properly for the important work we need them to do. They're essentially the reason we make so much progress here during the summers. We organise them into groups of six to twenty and assign them to particular digs.

"There will also be tour groups coming to participate in afternoon or day-long digs, and we help with those too. We have several projects on the go. I'll give you a run-down tomorrow morning and we can discuss where you'll be working."

"Sounds good." Sara applied her attention to her plate and as she ate, she listened with amusement to the good-natured banter between Thomas and his team. *He certainly seems to have a good rapport with everyone, from the dog to the cook to his subordinates. And he laughs a lot. His smile seems to light up his whole face and invite you to laugh along with him.*

She went to get a cup of chamomile tea, and when she returned, the fire had been lit and several people had produced musical instruments and were getting ready to play. Thomas was tuning an acoustic guitar, Patrick a banjo. Laura had a violin under her chin and Geoff was softly beating out a rhythm on bongo drums.

Dave played a few arpeggios on his bass guitar. "Let's start with 'Four Strong Winds'," he suggested. As the familiar tune filled the night air, Sara and the others began to sing.

chapter

FIVE

Bright sunlight slanted in the east window of the field office, lending a cheery air to the otherwise plain room. Thomas slid the window open with a sharp push, letting in the fresh morning air and the songs of the wrens in the cottonwoods. He pulled a manila file folder from the filing cabinet and handed it to Sara. "Here you go. This is the latest field report. It'll give you a run-down of our current activities."

He regarded Sara thoughtfully as she opened the file and scanned the contents. He hadn't been sure she would be ready to work this morning. She had disappeared into her tent last night, about an hour after the singing had started, claiming exhaustion.

Sorcha Lang

When she hadn't appeared at breakfast, he had assumed she was still catching up on sleep.

As it turned out, she had risen at the crack of dawn and had gone swimming in Sandhill Creek. Dave had told Thomas he'd seen her emerging from the water about the same time he was heading for the dining tent to start cooking.

"She's hot! Hot, hot, hot! So hot you'd think you need oven mitts to touch, but then you think the feel of that skin on bare hands might be worth the scalding if you scrapped the gloves," Dave had said as Thomas poured himself a cup of coffee. "I tell you, when I saw her dripping wet in that leopard print bathing suit, I wished I were drowning so that she would jump back in and rescue me. In fact, I plan to take up drowning first thing tomorrow morning. I'm even sure I'll need Sara to administer artificial respiration. Maybe she'll even have to take the suit off to use as a towing aid to get me to shore. And when we reach the bank, I'll...Ow! What'd you do that for?" He rubbed the ear Thomas had cuffed.

"Mind your manners," Thomas said. "Sara is here to work with dinosaurs, not to play around with little boys who are still in the drooling phase."

"You really mustn't talk about yourself in such a derogatory way," Dave said with an impudent grin. "Calling yourself a dinosaur when you've only just turned thirty. I mean, I'm not even sure people would place you in the Cretaceous period. I swear, Tom, you don't look a day older than 65 million. I'm sure that there must be some nice dinosauress from the Jurassic just waiting to make your acquaintance. But you can't have Sara. I called her first."

"Why did you call Sara?" Geoff joined them at the table. "She looked done in last night. She probably needs to sleep in today."

"Nah." Dave shook his head vigorously. "She was up before dawn. I was just explaining to my elderly cousin here, that Sara and I are a match made in heaven. That's because I, and I alone, know exactly what she needs, and it sure ain't dinosaurs. She needs youth, sex, excitement, joy, laughter, youth, sex—and did I mention youth and sex?"

"Yes, and you'd better not mention it again," Thomas said. "See you later, Geoff. I'll be at the quarry sometime before noon, I think. Dave, see me later about supplies—and try to stop drooling. I can't see Sara rescuing any dweeb drowning in his own saliva."

And now, looking across the desk at Sara, Thomas reflected that she didn't really look strong enough to rescue anyone from anything. She was pale, and her baggy cargo pants and loose shirt seemed to hang on her slender frame.

Too slender, as far as he was concerned. He wasn't particularly attracted to extreme thinness. He liked some softness to the female form. *She looks too fragile for palaeontology. She looks more like she should be growing roses in a conservatory or playing music in a symphony.* An image of her modelling a leopard skin bathing suit rose unbidden in his mind. Startled, he shook his head slightly. "Did you get any breakfast?"

Sara's head came up sharply. She still looked tired, with dark circles under her eyes, although the look she gave him was certainly very alert. "Of course. I like to be up for a while before I eat. When I can, I exercise first. That's a wonderful little stream behind the tents. I swam in it this morning."

"I heard." Thomas was careful to keep his tone neutral.

"Is that okay?" Sara seemed puzzled by his tone. "I ran into Dave and he didn't mention that there was any problem with my swimming in the stream."

"No, there's no problem," Thomas said. "In fact, you are probably setting a new trend. I fully expect the stream to be overflowing with bathers tomorrow morning."

"Oh, great! Very few of the palaeontologists I've worked with have shared my passion for swimming. Maybe we'll be able to give each other pointers or something."

"Or something." Thomas's tone was even drier. "Now about the report..."

Sara leaned forward eagerly. "I see you are currently working on several funding proposals. I could probably help, because I've done a lot of that sort of thing recently."

"Thanks for the offer, but I think we have the funding applications under control," Thomas said. "Patrick and I are handling it. What I really need—"

"But I have—" Thomas had raised his eyebrows and was looking at her inquiringly. Sara felt colour creep over her cheeks. She slid backward until she hit the chair back. "Sorry. Sometimes I get over-enthusiastic. Where would you like me to start work? I'm ready to begin right now."

Thomas frowned slightly and spun a pencil around his thumb. "Our main focus at the moment is to finish excavating the hadrosaur. It's encased in ironstone and is therefore quite well-preserved. We had thought to be finished with it by now, but bad weather has hampered our efforts.

"It's also been an extraordinary year for team injuries and health issues. As you're aware, Patrick's wife Mary is out because of her pregnancy; and then Gordon Spencer—do you know him?—fell on his way down a slippery cliff and broke his leg.

One other technician has a bad sprain and someone else contracted hepatitis..." He shook his head. "I've never seen anything like it.

"I spend most of my time with the hadrosaur team, but I have other commitments as well. I'll be away a couple of days at the upcoming Therapod Symposium. After that, I'll have to be away again for funding meetings. So, I could really use you at the hadrosaur quarry." He gave her a questioning look, "That is, if you're feeling up to it today?"

Sara could tell that Thomas doubted she'd be much use in the field. She had met this reaction before. People saw her slenderness, but overlooked her wiriness and knew nothing of her determination. It usually took a day or so in the field to change their opinions. *With Thomas, it will probably take at least a week.* "Of course I'm feeling up to it. I'd like to join the others as soon as possible."

"Right, then, let's go," Thomas stood and waited for her to precede him through the doorway. "Do you have a rucksack?"

"Yes." Most of the teams she had worked on supplied all the equipment, but she had a favourite rucksack she took with her on every expedition. It was strong, but light-weight, and had the right number of compartments for tools and snacks and anything else she needed.

"Okay," said Thomas. "Take whatever small tools you need from the shed attached to the office. I'll meet you in ten minutes at the dining tent, where we'll pick up our food and water. It's a forty-minute hike to the quarry."

"The dining tent in ten minutes. Okay." She headed to her tent as Thomas strode off in the opposite direction.

Fifty minutes later they were approaching the quarry. The team had rigged tarps in an attempt to provide some shade from what was promising to be a blistering summer sun. Barry and Mike were jackhammering away at some of the rock face and Samantha and Rob were trundling wheelbarrows full of rock and clay. Others were shovelling huge clumps of dirt and debris into five-gallon buckets.

Sara felt the stirrings of excitement that always appeared with the first dinosaur of the season. *And such a perfect glorious morning to be bringing this magnificent creature back into the light of day.* Her pace quickened. Thomas's strides also lengthened, as if the duckbilled dinosaur were some gigantic magnet inexorably drawing them in.

"We've made some headway, Tom," called Alan. "We've exposed the skull."

Laura looked up from where she was chipping away with a hammer and chisel at rock surrounding the tail. "C'mon over, Sara. There's plenty to do over here."

Sara joined Laura at the tail end and began to pick at the rock. As she hammered and whisked, Laura said, "We've had to remove tons of overburden to get to the bone-bearing layer. It's been very slow going, but we're getting there. If the weather holds—and they are forecasting sun for the next week or so—we might be finished in a couple of weeks."

She glanced up at the cloudless sky. "They're forecasting 48 degrees in the sun today and the sun is obviously where we're going to be. Thomas is always concerned about heatstroke, so make sure you pace yourself properly and take lots of water or he'll be after you."

They worked in companionable silence as the sounds of the dig filled the air around them. As usual, Sara lost herself in the rhythm picking away at sand and clay, chiselling stone, and whisking away dirt and dust. She liked the precision work of freeing the bone from the rock.

As she poured some acryloid onto the fragile bone to solidify and preserve it, her thoughts drifted to something she had read somewhere about Michelangelo. The great Renaissance sculptor had reportedly said that when he sculpted, he was merely freeing the form that was already present in the rock. *Just like palaeontology.*

The forms that she was helping to resurrect were, in her opinion, every bit as graceful and beautiful as Michelangelo's *Rondanini Pietà*.

Sara was roused from her reverie when someone called her name. She looked up, a little disoriented, to find Thomas looming over her.

"Don't you think it's time you took a break?" he said. "It's long past lunch. You need to get something to eat and to drink some water."

Sara glanced over at Laura, who shrugged. "I called you several times, but you were so engrossed in your work, you didn't even hear me. I don't think I've ever seen anyone work with that kind of concentration."

"Sorry. When I get focussed, you could drop a bomb beside me and I wouldn't hear it." She accepted the water bottle that Thomas was offering her and drank all of it. She hadn't realised she was so parched.

When she got up to get something to eat, her leg muscles protested at being stretched out of their cramped position. She limped over to her rucksack and pulled out her cheese sandwich.

Ten minutes later she was back to chiselling around the tail of the duck-billed dinosaur. And what seemed like ten minutes after that, the team called it a day and began to pack up.

The tarps were pulled down and the tools would be carted back to the field station.

Thomas fell into step beside her. "We're having more and more trouble with thieves and vandals. Too many of our fossils are ending up on the black market and in the hands of private collectors. So we don't like to leave too many pointers for poachers."

Sara was too tired to make conversation. All she could think about during the tiring trek back to camp was a quick dip in the stream, followed by a nice soothing shower before falling into bed. *One good thing about fieldwork is that if I work hard enough, I might actually sleep for most of the night.* She was a great believer in the benefits of a good night's sleep. Mostly because she rarely, if ever, got one. Her personal nightmares followed her wherever she went, and she was all too familiar with the negative effects of prolonged bouts of insomnia.

When she got back to the camp, many of the team members were cooling off in the stream, and she decided to join them. Feeling totally refreshed after a twenty-minute swim, she pulled herself up on the bank, where Patrick was towelling off.

"I haven't had a chance to talk to you all day. How'd you make out today?" he said.

"Oh, fine," Sara said. "I'm always most tired on the first day of a dig. Tomorrow'll be a lot better. But I did want to talk to you about my assignment."

Patrick frowned slightly. "Oh? Thomas is the one who does the assigning. If you're not happy with the job you've been given, maybe you should talk to him."

"I am happy," Sara hastily assured him. "I don't have a problem with my assignment. I'll keep working with everyone on the hadrosaur. It's just that I'd like to help out with other things too. Thomas mentioned that you and he are busy writing up funding proposals."

"Yeah. There are quite a few and it's taking an inordinate amount of time. I don't know how your funding is handled down east, but out here the government has moved to a matching funds system. We have to have all of our private funding secured before the government contributes a penny. And, of course, the more money we raise through alternate sources, the more the government will add to the coffers."

He stopped to towel dry his hair, and then continued. "What it means in practical terms is that we spend more than half our time trying to raise money instead of doing our jobs. The process is so complicated and the competition for limited funds so stiff, that you practically need a full-time person just to handle funding applications—and they'd better have a doctorate in grant applications."

Sara smiled sympathetically. "Believe me, I know. What are you applying for right now?"

"Well, the deadline for the Palaeontology and Archaeology Institute proposals is coming up quickly, so that's the one we're focussing on right now."

"Yes, well," Sara began, "I filled out the PAIN proposal for Andrew and when I spoke to the directors, they told me about some discretionary funds that are available. There's a sizable amount of money available if people would only apply for it. We could sit down together and I could go over it with you if you like."

"Good idea." Patrick slung his towel over his shoulder. "Let's talk about it later, okay? We should be able to find some time in the next couple of weeks. I'll ask Thomas what suits him.

Right now, it's almost time for supper. Are you going to shower before we eat?"

Sara grimaced as Patrick walked off towards the showers. Then she too headed in the same direction.

I wonder if I should have told him that Thomas has already as much as told me to butt out.

chapter

SIX

The next day dawned bright and clear. Sara pulled on her spare swimsuit, a high-cut black maillot, embroidered with a single golden sheaf of wheat that followed the curves of her torso. As she exited her tent, she nearly tripped over Barney, who was lying across the entrance. He wagged his tail and hopped up to accompany her to the stream, where he opted not to swim, but instead ran in and out among the cottonwoods, barking at some yellow warblers.

To her surprise, most members of the team were already in the stream—a change from the day before when she had been the lone swimmer. She entered slowly from the bank, feeling with her feet for the drop off point, and then quickly submerged her entire body in the cool water, which nevertheless felt warmer than the surrounding air. When she surfaced, she saw Dave busily trying to dunk Thomas while simultaneously fending off Mike.

When Thomas eluded Dave and swam to greet her, she said, "You and Dave should have come yesterday. I swam past that curve and I saw two mule deer drinking—a doe and her fawn."

His eyes twinkled as he pushed Dave away with one hand. "Did you? I'm not sure that that would interest Dave. I seem to recall his telling me that he is on the look-out for leopards today."

Sara returned his carefree smile. "Leopards? Dave, are you sure you're on the right continent? I've heard of the odd moose, and maybe a bobcat or two, but I've never heard of leopards in Dinosaur Provincial Park."

Dave's gaze was glued to Sara as she stepped onto a submerged rock and pulled her wet hair back in a ponytail. He whistled. "I'm a big big fan of leopards on *any* continent. I really like the tawny ones, but basic black is good, in fact very good. We could go leopard-hunting together, you know. Tan or black, doesn't matter to me. I'll quit my day job—" The rest of his sentence was drowned as Thomas ducked him under the surface.

Dave came up spluttering. He shrugged at Sara and said, "Sorry to abandon you, but my presence is urgently required elsewhere. A matter of revenge." He started after Thomas, whose strong strokes had already taken him to the bend in the stream.

After breakfast, as they began the morning hike to the hadrosaur quarry, Sara fell into step with Samantha and Laura.

At the quarry the men were already staking the tarps for the makeshift sun shelters. The women dropped their rucksacks

Love in the Age of Dinosaurs

in a heap and separated to continue the tasks they had been working on the previous day.

And so they continued for the next eleven days. Each scorching day melted into the next, until Sara had altogether lost track of time. The cycle repeated itself over and over with the rising and setting of the sun: morning swim, breakfast, trek, shovelling, picking, chiselling, whisking, gluing, mapping, photographing—all accompanied by a fair amount of nagging by Patrick and Thomas to take breaks. And then the trek back, followed by swimming, supper, music, bed.

The pattern continued without variation until at last, on the twelfth day, they were all ready, as Tom put it, "to get plastered". They had isolated each bone or group of bones on an island of sediment surrounded by trenches. Now Samantha and Geoff wrapped tissue around the bones and damped it with a wet brush to create a separator between the fossil and the layers of plaster which they were ready to apply.

As Sara dipped strips of burlap into wet plaster and then placed them over the tissue barrier, she thought about how she'd like to take a closer look at the area around the hadrosaur site. She had a hunch that there was more to discover. She'd had similar premonitions before and she'd learned to pay attention to them because most of the time they paid off.

There won't be much opportunity to look today because we still have to finish tunnelling under the bones and give the base its jacket. Nevertheless, the plaster would dry quickly in the hot desert-like conditions. By the next day they'd be able at last to exhume the bones from the sedimentary grave where they had been entombed for at least 65 million years.

Patrick had secured the services of a local trucking company to assist with the extraction and transport to the museum in Drumheller. Johnson's Trucking was scheduled to arrive from Brooks by ten o'clock and their equipment would greatly expedite the whole process of bone removal. Nevertheless, it would probably still take several hours to remove the bones. Sara knew from experience that the entire team was bound to be exhausted at the end of it.

The palaeontologists, having been through the process many times before, had prevailed upon everyone in camp to assist. The uninitiated agreed with alacrity; the experienced were a little more reluctant.

"Dave," Patrick said to Sara and Laura, "was not as enthusiastic as one could have wished, and it took a bit of convincing to get him here. If it hadn't been for good old Barney, who came bounding out of the trees at just the right moment, he might actually have gotten away from us."

"What happened?" said Laura. "You didn't press-gang him, did you?"

"No, I wouldn't call it that. We didn't use coins or anything."

"What exactly *did* you use?" Sara raised her eyebrows.

"Well, brute force, mostly. He was running away and Barney was running after a hare. Dave happened to be looking over his shoulder just when Barney bounded out from behind a bush. Barney was fixated on the hare, who was escaping from him; Dave was fixated on Tom, who was gaining on him. Luckily, Barney and Dave sort of collided. It didn't slow the dog down, but Dave tripped, and Tom was able to tackle him."

He chuckled. "Then Barney gave up on the hare and came and sat on Dave's chest, licking his face while we tied him up. We were just throwing him into the back of the Jeep and he was screaming like a banshee that he was being kidnapped, when some tough-looking tourists from the public campground happened by and asked us what was going on." Patrick laughed again. "I'm sure they thought we really were kidnapping him."

"Well, you were," Samantha said.

"Well, yeah, I suppose you could look at it that way. But Thomas set their minds at rest by explaining that Dave is an actor auditioning for a role with the Rosebud Theatre, and that we were rehearsing a kidnap scene with him. So they let it go. Patted Dave on the back and told him they hope he gets the part."

"Is Dave okay?" Sara said, with a smile twitching at the corners of her mouth.

"Oh, he's in fine form, threatening to poison us all at supper tonight. But Tom punched him on the shoulder and said that if he's a good boy and works hard, we can have a wiener roast instead." Still chuckling, he turned to leave, adding, "The kid actually is a good worker, you know. He just needs a little friendly persuasion now and again."

The exhausting work of removing the bones continued into mid-afternoon. Finally, the men attached cables to the wooden frames they had fastened to the plaster jacket, winched the main block out of the ground, and lifted it onto the back of the flatbed truck. Other, smaller, pieces, which were wrapped and tagged separately, were placed in labelled boxes and loaded as well. Further work to extricate the bones from the remaining matrix, as well as extensive tests and mounting, would be done in the museum lab, but for now the work at the quarry was finished.

Everyone cheered as the truck disappeared down the dusty track. They called it a day and began packing up the equipment to take back to camp.

chapter

SEVEN

"Coming, Sara?" Alan called. They were the last to leave the quarry. "I'm ready for a cool dip in the stream."

Sara looked up from her rucksack. She was busily trying to stuff a small tarp into the main compartment, which was already overcrowded with all of her usual tools, plus the consolidants—acryloid and paleobond—and a hand-held global positioning system which the others had left behind. She started to nod, but then hesitated.

"Y'know, I think maybe I'll hang around just a bit longer. I want to take my time and have a closer look around. I just have a feeling..."

Sorcha Lang

"I think the kit with the ground penetrating radar is back at the field station," Alan said. "And we're all tired. Why don't you leave it 'til tomorrow?"

Sara briefly considered the suggestion. She didn't want to offend Alan by rejecting his suggestion out of hand, but she rarely used GPR and she didn't want to wait until the next morning. She preferred to do things the old-fashioned way by trusting to instinct, observation, and a bit of luck. Besides, it wouldn't be dark for hours and her desire to re-examine the hadrosaur quarry was growing too strong for her to postpone it any longer. The quarry would be on her mind all night anyway and she wouldn't be able to sleep. So it really didn't make any difference whether she worked on it now or later. Either way, she'd be exhausted the next day.

She said slowly, "No, you know what? I think I'd like to do it without the GPR. But you go ahead and join the others. I shan't be too long, and you know where I am if anyone needs me."

Alan looked as though he were about to say something else, but he nodded in assent, and headed up the trail.

Sara walked back to the quarry and sat down to think. Before digging, she liked to picture a space as it would have been in the Cretaceous era—a large inland sea, lush forests, steamy tropical swamps, lots of tree ferns—and she liked to imagine how it would have felt to be a dinosaur at that time.

An hour or so later, her examination centred on an area some metres from where the hadrosaur's left tibia had lain. It was fairly easy to dig in the fine-grained rock. After a while, she switched from the shovel to a trowel and began to scrape very carefully at the soil. Within minutes, the tool hit something hard.

Sara carefully removed more of the earth, barely daring to breathe. More hard material. She used her whisk to brush away the soil and started scraping with an X-acto knife. She began to smile. She was onto something good here. She could just feel it in her bones.

After some time, she realised she was uncovering a skull. She wasn't entirely sure whether it was a bird or a dinosaur. She continued to work until, a few hours later, she had uncovered the well-preserved lower brain case of a skull. She was almost afraid to believe it was a *Troodon*. She took the reading from the GPS.

She photographed the skull from every conceivable angle, and took detailed field notes, including schematic drawings, recorded details of the geographic and stratigraphic locality, and documented the methods and materials she had used to uncover the fossil.

Thomas arrived just as she finished mapping her find. The feeling of being watched slowly crept over her, and she looked up. He was standing a few feet away.

"Oh! How long have you been there?"

"Long enough." He knelt beside her and examined the fossil. He gave a long low whistle. "It looks like *Troodon*. If so, this is the most complete specimen I've ever seen. We'll know for sure in a few days when we've had a chance to prepare it."

He looked at the sun's position, very low on the horizon. "Very impressive work, Sara." He extended his hand and pulled her to her feet. "But maybe it's time to call it a day. Let's cover it now, and we can plaster it tomorrow."

"I just need to apply some acryloid first," Sara said.

"I'll do it." Thomas applied the consolidant carefully so it didn't drip onto the surrounding matrix.

"Okay. I'll record it." Sara watched his deft movements. *Nice hands. Strong and capable, with slim, sensitive-looking fingers.*

Thomas glanced up and she quickly recorded the application of acryloid in her field notes.

Together they positioned the tarp from Sara's rucksack over the find and fastened it down with some tent pegs from the depths of her pack.

Thomas raised an eyebrow as he took note of the range of equipment Sara had managed to stuff into her bag. "Looks like you're a one-person excavation team. Were you planning an extended stay here on your own?" His smile changed to a frown pretty quickly, though, when he discovered her empty water bottle. "No water? When was the last time you had anything to drink?"

"About half an hour ago." Sara didn't quite meet Thomas's eyes. It wasn't exactly a fib. A half-hour previously she had tried to eke out the last bit of moisture from the bottle by shaking it over her open mouth, and a single drop had landed on her tongue. She didn't think anything was to be gained by telling Thomas, though, so she didn't elaborate, and she certainly wasn't going to mention her raging headache either.

He gave her a long look. "One of these days very soon, you and I are going to have a nice long chat about proper safety precautions in the field and honesty being the best policy." He paused. "I expect I'll enjoy it more than you will."

Sara wisely kept her own counsel on the silent march back to the camp.

chapter

EIGHT

The sky had lost its rosy streaks by the time Sara and Thomas arrived back at the camp, and in the darkness, the air had become quite cool. A large bonfire was snapping and cracking in the fire pit, and the aroma of cooked hotdogs wafted through the air. Sara dropped her gear off in her tent and returned to the warmth of the flames. When Geoff handed her a long green branch that he had sharpened to a point, she speared a raw wiener and stuck it in the fire and slowly rotated it.

"It'll turn black if you leave it there much longer," Thomas said. He was carefully roasting his own.

"That's the goal. I like it black on the outside. When we were kids, we'd—" She pulled the wiener back out of the fire. "I believe you're right. It's done. Are the buns in the dining tent?"

"Yes." Thomas watched Sara thoughtfully as she entered the dining tent in search of buns and condiments. For a fleeting instant before she had pulled her wiener from the fire, he could almost have sworn he had caught a flicker of sadness cross her face. It was gone so quickly that he couldn't be sure it wasn't just the play of light and shadow from the fire. He started to follow her, but paused when someone called his name. By the time he made his way to the dining tent, Sara had vanished. He stood at the entrance, trying to guess which way she had gone.

"There you are." Patrick appeared with his banjo in his hand. "Let's start the music, Tom. Everyone's so tired that we'll probably all be falling into the flames before much longer. Where'd Sara go?"

"I don't know. Maybe to bed. At least I hope so. Did you know she stayed up at the quarry after everyone left?"

Patrick raised his eyebrows. "No, actually, I didn't. What was she doing?"

Thomas filled Patrick in on Sara's find.

Patrick whistled. "Well, that's our Sara," he said. "She sees things that others don't, keeps plugging away when others quit—" He must have noticed the expression on Thomas's face. "You don't look particularly happy."

"I'm all for discovering fossils, Pat. I just don't like the idea of people killing themselves in the process. Has anyone ever tried to teach Sara how to pace herself?"

Patrick groaned. "Not a task for the faint of heart, that one. We've all had a go at it, but she's got a mind of her own, you know. Somehow, everything we say falls on deaf ears. She ends up doing as she pleases."

Thomas raised an eyebrow, but said nothing more. They walked back towards the fire and the soft strumming of Dave's guitar.

Sara could hear strains of music as she walked along the stream. Still too keyed up from the excitement of her find at the quarry, she needed to burn off some of her excess energy before she tried to sleep. Her headache had finally subsided. Barney trotted along behind her, sniffing at every leaf and investigating every tree. After thirty minutes, she turned back towards camp. The music had ended and it appeared that everyone had gone to bed. She had almost reached her own tent when a tall shadow loomed beside her and someone grasped her lightly by the arm.

"Out for a midnight stroll?" Thomas's voice was soft.

Sara couldn't see his face clearly. She thought he sounded tired, though. "Oh, Thomas, I'm sorry. Were you looking for Barney? He just followed me. I'm always keyed up after a fossil find and I needed to unwind a bit before bed, so I went for a walk along the stream. Before I knew it, Barney was trotting along behind. But I think he's ready to settle down now and so am I. I'm totally exhausted." She turned to unzip her tent. "Good night. I'll see you tomorrow."

"Sure. There's always tomorrow. We can talk then."

Not if I can bloody well avoid it.

chapter

NINE

By the time Sara appeared at the stream the following morning, news of her find had spread amongst the team.

"Wow, Sara," Samantha said. "How did you know where to look without the GPR?"

"Oh, I don't know. I just had a feeling there might be something there and—"

"A feeling?" Samantha was clearly impressed. "We're going to have to start calling you 'Sue'."

Sara smiled uneasily. She felt Thomas watching her and she tried to think of a way to change the topic. Her hunches sounded so idiotic when discussed in the cold light of day. She was supposed to be a scientist, supposed to accept that the scientific method involved empirical observation, not wishy-washy techniques like following hunches. True scientists weren't supposed to have time for fuzzy concepts like women's intuition or feelings of *déjà vu*. She was willing to bet her soul that Thomas would think such things utter rubbish.

"Sue?" Rob sounded mystified.

"Sue *Hendrickson,* dude," said Mike, as he exchanged a glance with Thomas. "You know...Think *T. rex*..."

"Oh, *that* Sue." Rob groaned.

"Who is Sue?" Dave said. "Is she someone I should meet?"

"Sue Hendrickson," explained Barry, "is arguably the most famous amateur palaeontologist on the planet. She is responsible for the discovery of the most complete *Tyrannosaurus rex* skeleton ever found. And it was all just because of a *feeling* she had about a certain cliff she had seen."

Mike said, "She was with some fossil hunters in South Dakota. They'd had a fairly productive summer and were packing up. Something happened to their truck—a flat tire or something—"

Alan broke in. "—and the spare was low on air, so—"

Rob picked up the story. "So the team headed to a service station, but Sue stayed behind, and got to thinking about a cliff she had seen and hadn't had time to explore. She and her dog hiked seven miles to the cliff."

"At the base," Thomas said, "she found some pieces of bone. As any well-trained palaeontologist should do, she looked up to locate the source of the bones. About seven feet up the cliff face, she saw three vertebrae sticking out. And the rest, as they say, is history. The team spent three weeks digging out the most complete skeleton of *T. rex* currently in existence."

Love in the Age of Dinosaurs

"It was in the papers for ages," Alan said, "and not just because it was a spectacular find. There was a huge battle over ownership among the U.S. government, the Sioux Indians, and the land-owner—a guy named Williams. Eventually, the courts awarded ownership to Williams. He sold the skeleton at auction. The Field Museum in Chicago bought it for over eight million dollars. And, of course, the dinosaur's nickname is 'Sue'."

"And is it 'A Boy Named Sue'?" Dave said with a laugh.

"All we know is that the growth rings in the bone show that it was 29 when it died, making it the oldest known *T. rex*, and that it lived a rough life, survived fractures, and had a bacterial infection."

"And we know Sue Hendrickson has quite a history of finding things through a…Well, for lack of a better word…sixth sense," Rob said. "She's been involved in the discovery of a slew of things—butterfly fossils, buried treasure, Cleopatra's palace, Napoleon's sunken warships. She's pretty amazing, actually."

"So, Sara." Dave turned to where she'd been standing. "Hey, where's Sara?"

"She got out a while ago," Thomas said. "She said she felt really cold today and was going to cut it short."

"And I missed it. While I was focussed on the past, the present passed me by." He shook his head as he got out of the water, grumbling all the while about missing his opportunity to spend time with Sara. He stomped around the kitchen tent, not accomplishing much.

Eventually Thomas tired of his tantrum. "At present, there are seven hungry males waiting to eat. Regardless of the past, if breakfast doesn't appear very soon, you may never experience a future."

57

After breakfast a few members of the team headed back to the quarry with Sara to finish excavating the *Troodon* skull. Some of them would use the GPR or reconnoitre to see if they could find other bones of the *Troodon*.

They had been supposed to have the day off because of the long hours and the number of days they had worked without a break. But removal of the *Troodon* skull was a priority, since meteorologists were predicting thundershowers by late afternoon or evening. Thomas estimated they would be finished by noon, so they could relax for the remainder of the day.

He looked up enquiringly when he heard Patrick laugh.

"I don't know that Mike is really all that enthralled with the contents of her notebook," Patrick explained. "Sara is so wrapped up in palaeontology that it never occurs to her that guys are interested in anything else."

"Judging from the conversation, I think Mike actually is interested in the palaeontology," Thomas said. "At least for the moment. That's some fascinating journal she keeps. Geoff, Rob, Barry, and Alan are all infatuated with it too."

Patrick laughed again. "Sounds like you're keeping a close eye on Sara."

"I don't need to keep a close eye on Sara, Pat. I just have to locate the long line of salivating males to know where she is. Maybe she doesn't need to be quite so generous with her time and expertise."

"Sara's always generous with everything and everyone," Patrick said. "Male or female. Have you seen how much Sam and Laura have improved at swimming? That's mostly because Sara has been helping them and she always devotes herself wholly to the task at hand."

Thomas conceded. "There's never anything half-hearted about Sara's efforts. That's partly why she's such a good palaeontologist. That and her tremendous natural ability, of course." The conversation died away as he and Patrick focussed on their work, but his thoughts remained centred on Sara.

For all her talent as a palaeontologist, she had so far shown no natural ability for self-preservation. She drove herself too hard, she didn't take enough breaks, and she didn't take the necessary personal safety precautions while working on site. She was always forgetting to drink while she worked, and on at least one occasion, she hadn't brought any lunch. That kind of behaviour could only have negative effects on her health. Heat stroke was a serious threat in the short term, and in the long term, she was at risk of burning herself out completely.

He wondered briefly if Andrew Turner, Sara's supervisor on the east coast, had had similar concerns about her. He also wondered if Sara had told him as many blatant untruths as she had told Thomas. He smiled wryly and shook his head.

She seems to think that she can pull the wool over my eyes. She always says she's had enough water, food, rest, whatever. It might be time to call her in for that little chat he had promised they were going to have.

The excavation proceeded smoothly and quickly, thanks mostly to the small size of the fossil and the incredible amount of work that Sara had done on the previous day. No other fossils were uncovered and some of the team started drifting back to the camp. Only a few were left to make desultory conversation as they finished packing up.

Mike, who appeared increasingly impressed by the calibre of Sara's work, asked Thomas, "Did you see her field notes? They're amazingly complete and they're still in rough form. She records everything—all the usual information, plus every tool used, every application of paleobond or acryloid. I wonder why she doesn't use a laptop, though. I've seen her transferring her notes to the computer in the lab."

"Yes, she's meticulous." He too had wondered about the lack of a personal computer. It seemed slightly out of character for her to arrive at a palaeontology project without a laptop. Not that a laptop would be much use if she wanted to use the internet in Dinosaur Provincial Park. Even cell phones didn't work in here. Still, a laptop would be useful for note-taking and word processing.

"Sara," Mike called. "Where's your laptop? Don't you have one?"

Sara looked over and shrugged. "I didn't bring it with me. I'm leaving on holiday right after I'm done here, and I didn't want to lug it around." She saw no reason to mention that her boss had confiscated all of her equipment before she'd left. She hadn't even had time to save anything on the flash drive so she could transfer material to her home computer. Not that it would have made any difference, since he'd taken the flash drive too. And she'd not been able to object; the laptop and all of its accessories were owned by the museum.

Sara noticed an expression of scepticism on Thomas's face. *Drat the man! It's as if he can see right through me.* She continued virtuously, "I never mix business with pleasure and I never ever take a laptop or cell phone on holidays with me." *It's not a lie, because I never take holidays. But if I did, I wouldn't take any work along.*

She leaned towards Mike. "I think it's a crying shame that so many people can't separate leisure time from work time, don't you? My boss and I discuss that issue all the time." She lowered her gaze demurely, although she shot a glance in Thomas's direction to measure his response.

Thomas merely grinned and lowered his left eyelid in a slow, and—in Sara's opinion—malicious, wink. In a conversational tone, he said, "I don't know if I mentioned it before, Sara, but Andrew Turner e-mailed me that he'll be in Calgary next week. Let me know if you have any messages you'd like me to pass on when I see him."

Sara slammed shut her hard-backed field journal and jumped to her feet. "Right. Well, I guess we're done here. C'mon, Laura, let's go. See you back at camp."

Mike raised his eyebrows questioningly, but Thomas merely grinned and said, "I hope it was nothing I said..."

Sara could hear the laughter in Thomas's voice as she stomped up the trail with Laura in tow. "That insufferable man!" she fumed. "He didn't believe a word I said."

"Of course he did," Laura said in a soothing tone. "Why wouldn't he believe you? It's not as if you've made a habit of lying to him, is it? I mean, apart from those times you claimed you'd taken adequate breaks...Oh, and I guess there were a few times when you went out prospecting on your own and told me to say you were in the showers. And then there was that day you forgot your lunch and didn't tell anyone. But apart from those, you haven't told any other lies, have you?" She stopped walking and gave Sara a questioning look. "Come to think of it, Sara, maybe—"

"That is not the point," Sara said. "He should at least look like he believes me when I tell him things. It's just plain rude to raise your eyebrow at people and give them mocking looks."

She turned to glower at Laura. "Don't you think it's obnoxious to advertise your doubts about someone's honesty?" She didn't wait for Laura's response. "Well, let me tell you, I find it highly objectionable." She stomped up the path, knowing Laura was grinning as she followed.

It took an heroic effort, but, eventually, Sara managed to control her irritation. "Never mind. It's too nice a day to spend worrying about what 'Doubting Thomas' thinks."

If he thinks!

After a quick swim Laura returned to the camp, claiming she wanted to finish the mystery she was reading. Feeling restless, Sara decided to take a walk along the stream. She put a few things in a cotton bag and slung it over her shoulder before sauntering down to the water where she strolled along the bank. After a while, she settled herself under a cottonwood, took out her camera and placed it on the ground within easy reach. She opened a paperback, and began to read.

Half an hour later, her stillness was rewarded by the arrival of a Great Blue Heron on the opposite bank. It stood motionless for a few moments, and then stepped daintily over to the water. Sara groped for her camera, and keeping her eyes on the bird, slowly lifted the camera to her face, focussed on the heron—and took a picture of the sky.

Barney's enthusiastic arrival had literally bowled her over and she snapped just at the point the camera was pointed directly overhead. She pushed the dog off her chest. "Barney! Why did you have to do that?"

Thomas appeared, laughing. "Sorry about that. He's apparently very happy to find you." He pulled the dog away, as he kept trying to climb back onto Sara's lap. "Hasn't it been all of a couple of hours since he last saw you?"

"Something like that." She reached out to pet Barney, who started to wag his tail so vigorously that she thought it might be in danger of falling off.

Thomas sat down beside Sara. "So what is it about you, Sara? You're a magnet for this dog. Before you came, he was glued to me. Now I'm starting to think I'll die of loneliness if I don't get another pet to keep me company while you're around. Are there any other animals I could latch onto without fear of your stealing their hearts away?"

"Well," said Sara modestly, "as you can see, the birds are pretty wary. That blue heron is probably gone forever."

"How about cats?"

"No, a cat is definitely not a good choice. For reasons unknown, cats appear to like me very much." She started to laugh. "One time at Alex's music lesson—" She closed her mouth abruptly and stood. "It looks like it's going to rain. Maybe we should go back to the camp."

"Sure. Let's go. C'mon Barney."

They started back towards camp.

"By the way," Thomas said, deliberately casual, "who is Alex?"

chapter

TEN

Thomas knew Sara did not want to answer his question. She had stiffened when he asked it. And she was taking an awfully long time to answer. Somewhat to his own surprise, he wanted an answer and he was going to get one, even if he had to wait for it.

He waited.

Finally, Sara said, "My brother."

Thomas suddenly felt like singing, but he took the hint, and quietly changed the subject. Sara was obviously reluctant to talk about her brother, and he had no intention of forcing her to. Instead he sought out Patrick, who was relaxing in the shade with a cold beer and a newspaper. Thomas went and got a beer for himself, and sat down. "We need to talk about Sara."

Patrick directed a level look at him. "What do you need to know?"

"Anything you can tell me. All I know is that she's a talented palaeontologist, a workaholic, a good swimmer, a personable team-member, and my dog's best friend." He took a sip of beer. "And that she has a brother named Alex."

Patrick sighed. "*Had* a brother named Alex."

Thomas raised an eyebrow.

"It's a sad story. Sara never talks about it, so if you're to know, I guess you'll have to hear it from me." He paused, as if trying to decide where to begin. "She's originally from Edmonton. Her father was a doctor; her mother a geologist. She had one brother, Alex, five years her junior. She adored him. The family was very close, especially the two kids. Alex was a talented musician, particularly on the piano. He was quite a character—cheerful and happy-go-lucky. Dave reminds me a lot of Alex." He paused and grimaced. "Five years ago, the whole family died in a car crash caused by a drunk driver. Sara was supposed to have been in the car, too, but she was working late in the university lab, and ended up not going with them. And so she was spared."

Thomas didn't know quite what he had expected to hear, but it certainly wasn't this.

Patrick continued, "After that, Sara didn't stick around much longer. She headed out to Australia first, and then wound up in the States. She's been on the east coast for the last few years. Mary and I have been pressing her to return to Canada, but the answer has always been a definite no. When I suggested she come out here for a few weeks this summer, at first she said no, that she wasn't ever returning to Alberta."

"So what made her change her mind?"

Patrick looked a little sheepish. "Well, I might have pressured her a little."

Thomas asked, "A little?"

"Well, a lot, actually," admitted Patrick. "She's really not that hard to convince if you understand a few basic things about her."

"For instance?"

"For instance, Sara always roots for the underdog. So all you have to do is present someone in that light and Sara will immediately throw her support behind him. Then there's her love of palaeontology, which is a good lever, too. If it's for the good of her chosen profession, there isn't much she won't sacrifice. And, well, I'm ashamed to admit it, but her love and loyalty can also be used against her. There is nothing that she wouldn't do for me or Mary, which is why we make a point of never asking her for anything. So, when I practically begged her to come out here this summer, I knew she wouldn't be able to say no."

"I see," Thomas said slowly. "So let me see if I have this straight. She came because of her love for you and Mary, presumably because the need was great if you were actually desperate enough to ask her for a favour. That right?"

Patrick nodded.

"Then, when you informed her about our setbacks because of weather, illness, whatever, she was impelled to help out fellow palaeontologists due to professional loyalty. That right?"

Patrick nodded again.

"Okay," said Thomas. "The only thing I don't get is who the underdog is."

Patrick picked up his empty glass, and headed towards the dining tent. "Well, mate, I guess that'd be *you*."

Sorcha Lang

Thomas was on his feet in a flash. He started after Patrick, who seemed to have disappeared in an awful hurry, but found his way blocked by Dave and Alan. "Hey, Tom, where are you going? We've made plans and you're in them."

Thomas stared at them blankly. "What?"

"We figured there's no use just sitting around in our tents while it pours all night," Dave explained. "So we're all going into Brooks."

"What?" said Thomas again.

"The Greenwood Golf and Country Club is holding its annual old-fashioned country dinner tonight and you're invited. Smile, Tom, you're being taken for a ride and then you're going dancing!"

chapter

ELEVEN

"Have you ever heard of *The Silver Club Four?*" Sara asked Sam and Laura as they dressed in the women's shower room. "What kind of music do they play?"

"Well, I've never heard them perform," said Sam, "but I know they're a local group. There are four musicians, but I don't know what instruments they play."

Laura looked up from fastening her sandal. "Dave showed me a poster. I seem to remember a cute guy on piano, a drummer, and a sax player. The sax player is really hot. I think maybe the other guy was on guitar." She paused a moment to think. "Yeah, I'm sure he was on guitar, because I noticed it was a left-handed guitar, like Paul McCartney plays. From what I've heard, they're pretty good for a small-town band."

"So they're country and western?" Sara said.

"That I don't know. They might be a swing band. Dave said it's an old-fashioned country dinner and dance. I expect it'll be old time dances like our grandparents used to dance—things like polkas and waltzes."

Sara smiled at her reflection. "This is going to be such fun. I hope. What if the men are only interested in the dinner and not in the music? What if no one asks us to dance?"

Laura folded her arms and tapped her foot. "Well, there's nothing like looking on the bright side, Sara!"

Samantha finished applying lip gloss. "Relax. There's nothing to worry about. These are grown-up men with grown-up interests. They won't pass up an opportunity to strut their stuff and hold grown-up women in their arms. Besides, I've already made it very clear to at least some of the guys that a full dance card makes for a happy woman, and that a happy woman makes for a happy palaeontologist. I'm pretty sure they got my drift."

"It's pretty sad if we have to stoop to coercion," Sara had to say.

"It wasn't coercion. It was just a friendly hint." Sam adopted a pious tone as she examined her fingernails. "I like to do what I can to improve relations between the genders.

"And so," she went on, "although I think we should keep it open as a last resort, I don't think we'll actually have to break their arms to get them to dance with us. I just happened to overhear Dave telling Patrick to spread the word that he, Dave, had already reserved every waltz for Sara."

"Oh, really?" said Laura. "I think Thomas might have something to say about that."

"Now look what you've done, Sara," scolded Sam. "You've smeared your mascara right onto your eyebrow." She reached for a tissue and started dabbing at Sara's face. "Here, let me fix that."

She finished fussing and stood back for a critical look. "There. That's better." She exchanged a sly glance with Laura. "I don't think you'll need any rouge today. Your cheeks have gone quite pink. Don't you think she's cute when she's embarrassed, Laura?"

Laura nodded. "Oh, definitely. In fact, I think Thomas thinks she's cute all the time."

Sara put her hands up to her cheeks. They were hot to the touch. "I-I don't know what you mean."

Laura put her hands on her hips. "Face it, Sara. Our team leader is smitten. And you're the smiter."

"Well, if Thomas is smitten, he has a funny way of showing it. Honestly, you have no idea how that man treats me."

"Oh, we have plenty of ideas!" Laura grinned. "It's just you and Thomas who are clueless."

Sara gave her a stern look. "It's a mystery to me why you think there is, or ever could be, something between Thomas and me."

Laura just rolled her eyes. "C'mon. Let's go. We have an evening of serious playing ahead of us."

Thomas and me? Sara opened the Jeep door and took her seat beside Geoff. *As if! It seems like any time I'm around him, all he does is criticise. First the hitch-hiking, then how much water I drink, and when I drink it. And he's practically called me a liar. Sam and Laura are totally off base on this one. I don't think he likes me much at all, and as for me, I'd sooner spend time with Barney. At least Barney doesn't raise his eyebrow when I'm trying to tell him something!*

Thirty minutes later, they pulled into the parking lot at the Greenwood Golf and Country Club. "Well, I don't know if it looks like this in dry years, but it's certainly aptly named for this year," Geoff said.

Sara could only concur. The attractive grey fieldstone building was surrounded by a stunning tapestry of rich and varied tints of green interspersed with splashes of other colours. Silvery-green leaves of beautiful Russian olive trees and the shiny foliage of graceful weeping birch brushed the velvety carpet of emerald green grass. Dark green ivy covered the low stone wall and spilled over onto flagstone walkways bordered with forest green ferns, feathery flax, and intermittent sprays of brilliant red geraniums and purple and white petunias.

"It's so beautiful, I hate to go inside," she breathed. In the next instant, the plop of big, wet drops gave notice that the misty drizzle was turning into steady rain. She had to hurry in with the others to avoid getting drenched.

The foyer of the clubhouse was as attractive as the exterior. Stone plant-holders full of Boston ferns and Ming Aralias rose up out of the dark grey slate floor. Two wide oak doors in the centre hallway opened into a long room with floor to ceiling windows overlooking the golf course. A string quartet was playing classical music on the stage as ushers showed the guests to their seats at long tables covered with delicately embroidered tablecloths and matching napkins.

Soon after they were seated, the master of ceremonies stood up to welcome the guests and speak briefly about the Club's annual tradition of holding a country dinner and dance. He finished speaking to polite applause and then the quartet began to play again while waiters began serving the meal.

Love in the Age of Dinosaurs

It really was an old-fashioned country dinner. By the time Sara had finished the generous portions of roast beef and Yorkshire pudding, assorted vegetables and hot apple pie and ice cream, she was beginning to wonder if she would be able to move, let alone dance.

"Don't worry," said Laura, when she moaned about being full. "We have a bit of time before the dancing starts. Let's see if the rain has stopped. We can walk around a bit while they remove the tables and set up for the dance."

The rain had stopped, although everything was still dripping, so they were able to take a brief stroll in the gardens. When they returned, the dining room had been transformed. The string quartet was gone and The Silver Club Four were playing their first number, a two-step.

They were barely through the door before they were invited to dance. Sara danced the two-step with Alan and a one-step with Barry. Mike led her through a polka, and she jived with Dave. Through it all, she was conscious of Thomas dancing with other women. Like Dave, he was a brilliant dancer. *It's like Kelly said. He is a ten. Why do Sam and Laura think he likes me? They're the ones he keeps asking to dance.*

Finally, needing something to drink, she apologetically turned down another invitation to dance and made her way to the refreshment table. Thomas was ladling out a cup of punch, which he handed to Sara. He poured himself one as well.

They stood together, in companionable silence, sipping their drinks and watching the other dancers.

"Well, I'll say one thing for Dave," remarked Thomas after a while. "He does a mean fox-trot."

Sara looked over to where Laura and Dave were dancing. "You're right. He's good."

"Our grandparents—mostly my grandmother, I think—taught him how to dance."

"Were they professional dancers?"

"Oh, no. They were farmers." And he proceeded to amuse Sara with stories of his grandparents and their lives farming on the prairies after they had emigrated from Scotland.

"They were very poor during the Depression," he said, "but it didn't set them apart because everyone else was in the same boat. There was plenty to eat, of course, because they grew their own food. They, like all the other farmers in the area, often fed the hobos who rode the rails and turned up on their doorsteps needing a hot meal. There wasn't much money, though, for clothing or luxuries. No Christmas presents in the stockings—just nuts and cookies. But they had their fun. Every Saturday night there was a dance. That's why they were all such fabulous dancers.

"You know, I think tonight we stepped back in time and captured a bit of my grandparents' time. Not only the dance numbers, but the way the men and women arranged themselves on opposite sides of the room. My grandfather said all the men were terrified of asking a woman to dance and then being turned down. Grandmother said the women were all terrified that they wouldn't get asked to dance."

He smiled down at Sara and shook his head slightly, "Of course, some things have changed since then. The men are still worried about rejection, but the women don't seem to worry about being wallflowers."

"Oh, I guess," Sara murmured.

Dance followed dance until finally the band announced the final waltz of the evening. Dave was turning towards Sara, when Thomas spoke from behind her.

"This one is mine, I believe." He lightly grasped Sara's elbow and led her onto the floor.

Later, when the evening had ended and Sara was crawling into her sleeping bag, she smiled with pleasure as she recalled that last waltz with Thomas. It was purely and simply the best dance she had ever had in her life. It wasn't just that Thomas knew the steps; it was the way he held her in his arms, somehow managing to make her feel safe and cherished at the same time. He danced so effortlessly and so smoothly that she had simply closed her eyes and floated. A few beats into the music, he had tightened his hold.

As Sara melded to his body, they had moved as one. She had begun to feel that she'd like the dance to go on forever, but the music finally came to an end. She and Thomas had reluctantly moved apart.

He had looked as stunned as she felt. His "Thank you for the dance," echoed hers perfectly.

As she switched off her flashlight, and huddled deeper into her sleeping bag, Sara hugged to herself one last memory of the evening. Just before Thomas had let her go, she was almost sure she had felt his lips brush her hair.

chapter

TWELVE

The next morning, life returned to normal. It had stopped raining, but the air was damp and cool. At first Sara and Patrick were the only ones in the stream. Thomas turned up after a while, looking like he hadn't slept too well.

He was not particularly communicative and his response to Patrick's greeting was more a grunt than a hello.

Patrick merely grinned. "So are we still working on the funding forms before breakfast?"

"Yeah. Give me twenty minutes." He turned towards the bend in the stream.

Sara quickly turned in the opposite direction, intending to slip quietly away. Thomas appeared to be ignoring her, and given his present mood, the less attention she received, the better.

"And, Sara—"

She stopped dead.

"Don't think I've forgotten about our chat. See me in my office after breakfast."

Sara strode to the shower room, muttering to herself. "It's as if last night never happened. I must have imagined it. Maybe there was something in the punch, or maybe I was just so tired at the end that I imagined—"

She stumbled on a stone, slightly twisting her ankle. "Ouch! So far, this is not turning out to be a great morning. So, Sara Wickham, forget about Thomas the ogre, stop mooning about, and start watching where you're going."

Feeling simultaneously refreshed and warmed from her shower, Sara considered how to kill the time before breakfast. Dave was still abed, which meant she had at least two free hours before her meeting with Thomas. She could use that time profitably. She certainly had no intention of wasting it by cowering in her tent and biting her nails to the quick as she brooded about the coming interview.

This is a good opportunity to take a quick look at that area by the river. Besides, if I hang around here, I might run into Thomas again before he's eaten. And he might decide we have to talk before we eat and that I definitely do not want to do. I'd rather not converse with him at all this morning, much less on his empty stomach. Especially since I probably won't be able to get a word in edgewise. I'd bet my life he plans to do all the talking, and I somehow doubt it will be compliments on my dancing. Maybe he'll be in a better mood after breakfast.

Love in the Age of Dinosaurs

She stopped in her tent to grab her rucksack and some rain gear, and then ducked into the still-empty dining tent to grab an apple and some cheese. *This should tide me over until lunch, Funny how much hungrier I was before I ran into Thomas at the stream. Someone really ought to tell him that these little tête-à-têtes he's so fond of serve no purpose other than to ruin innocent people's appetites.*

She paused by Laura's tent on her way to the tool shed. *I should probably let someone know where I'm going, just in case. But I hate to wake anyone up just to say that I'm going for a brief walk. Everyone's tired and we rarely get a chance to sleep in. Besides, I'll be back long before anyone even notices I'm gone.*

She continued walking, impatiently brushing from her mind a tiny, tenacious tendril of concern about Thomas's likely reaction if he discovered that she had gone off on her own without informing anyone. *What could possibly happen in such a short time and so close to camp? Thomas won't even miss me.*

As she walked, what began as a slight drizzle turned into a torrential downpour. The only shelter around was a limestone-capped hoodoo. She huddled under it.

Not a bad umbrella at all. Funny that the Indians regarded hoodoos as evil. I've always thought of them as friendly, and having a sense of humour, with their jaunty tams. She cast her mind back, trying to recall what she knew about cultural beliefs surrounding hoodoos.

The word itself, she'd learned long before, was an old Hausa word meaning to "arouse resentment" or "produce retribution". *Extraordinary that a West African word found its way to North America in the eighteenth century and became a part of scientific vocabulary.* She knew that local aboriginal peoples had used the word to refer to evil, supernatural forces. Sara touched the grey sandstone. *Are*

Sorcha Lang

you really a giant turned to stone by the Great Spirit as punishment for your evil deeds?

If so, the giant had over time replaced malevolence with benevolence. *We all mellow over time.* And this hoodoo had been mellowing for a very long time. Ten thousand years of erosion had been slowed, but not stopped, by the protective cap.

She ran her fingers along the surface of the striated pillar and thought about the passage of time. The brown shale layer at the bottom had been the floor of the ancient sea that had covered the area around seventy-three million years before. That was the layer containing marine fossils. The upper gray sandstone section had been formed by sand deposited by rivers and streams approximately seventy million years ago—a time of swamps, lakes, forests, and dinosaurs.

Like the dinosaurs and their habitat, the hoodoo itself would eventually disappear. The softer rock beneath the capstone was constantly eroding, and when the caprock eventually fell, wind and water would quickly erode the unsheltered hoodoo until at last it vanished into oblivion.

But not today. That fate was for a distant future.

As Sara stood, mesmerised by the rain, the landscape surrounding the hoodoo began to change before her very eyes. Water splashed off rocks and formed rivulets on the ground, transporting particles of soil, creating tiny rills that, over eons, would evolve into gullies, ravines, canyons. The only dry and constant space was where she stood beneath the hoodoo, protected from the wind for a breathless instant when time itself seemed to pause and hold her suspended between two worlds.

In the fluid world around her, time ticked inexorably on and the living earth responded willingly and irrevocably to ageless agents of endless transformation.

Love in the Age of Dinosaurs

In the next instant Sara once again felt the breeze on her face and she re-entered the temporal world of flux and change.

At last the gray clouds started breaking up and moving off to the north. When Sara caught a glimpse of blue sky, she left the shelter of the hoodoo and continued in a southerly direction. She walked slowly, picking her way with care. Because the bentonitic clay had expanded as it absorbed water, the soil underfoot had become extremely slippery.

Eventually her perambulations took her closer to a bend in the Red Deer River, where a tantalising rise seemed likely to yield promising results. She clambered up the slope, eased her pack off her back, and took a single step backwards.

The wet ground gave way beneath her feet. Arms windmilling, she slid head over heels, in a shower of gravel and mud. Her fall ended in the bottom of a sinkhole.

She lay still for a few minutes, stunned. Once she was sure the hillside had stopped moving, she stood slowly, shaking her limbs to see if everything was intact. She took stock of her surroundings and ruefully realised that climbing out was not going to be easy.

She tried on each side of the sinkhole, but couldn't get a proper toe-hold and kept slipping back. Her body, front and back, was now streaked with mud. She would just have to wait and hope that once the bentonite had dried sufficiently, she would be able to crawl out. In the meanwhile, she'd take a closer look around.

She circled slowly around once again. The ground beneath her feet squelched a bit. She bent to pick up a rock, then quickly dropped it as a scorpion scuttled from underneath. She hugged herself tightly. *Ugh. Oh God, why did this have to happen? I hate scorpions. Where did it go?*

Off to the side, something pale slithered away and disappeared.

She shuddered. *What was that?*

A sob rose in her throat. She looked wistfully at the open sky so far above her. How could freedom be so apparent and so unattainable?

Don't think about it right now.

She looked down again and tripped over something hard before her eyes readjusted to the dimness. She squinted at the shape as she massaged her shin. She stiffened.

This is no ordinary rock.

She knelt close to it. "A vertebra. But of what?" The last two words echoed eerily off the walls.

Her hackles rose.

A sinkhole was a deathtrap.

Where there was one bone, there were bound to be others. Many animals would have been lured down into the waterhole. Few would ever have made their way out again.

The light shifted, dimmed. She crawled slowly around the bone, then widened her circle and crawled again. Finally, she felt something solid. She slid her hand along a bone that seemed to go on forever.

For the first time since her fall, Sara smiled. It was a femur.

A femur this large belonged to a very large carnivore.

She shook with excitement.

Could it be an *Albertosaurus*?

Sara sat back on her haunches. Where there was an *Albertosaurus,* there had to be other, smaller prey. She began to look for more dinosaurs.

Hours passed. Sara found many more bones. She tried and tried again to scale the walls of the sinkhole. Several times during the day, she thought she heard people calling her name, but when she called in reply, no one answered. By evening, she had screamed herself hoarse. Her throat ached and she longed for a drink of water. She huddled beneath the hole, watching the light diminish.

A sinkhole is a deathtrap.

"And that is quite enough of that, Sara Wickham. If you have any wits, it is time to use them. The soil will not get drier. Rescuers are not at hand. Get up and save yourself."

She began to crawl upwards. Almost every time she moved forward, she seemed to slip back just as far. Once, as she neared the top, she slid nearly to the bottom on her stomach, painfully scraping her left forearm. On her third try, she was reaching for a handhold when her wrist was firmly grasped, and someone began to haul her up.

Thank goodness. Now please let it not be—

Thomas gave a final yank that sent them both sprawling. For a few seconds they just stared in silence at one another.

"Uh…well, thanks," Sara finally managed.

His face had registered a swift range of emotions, including shock, concern, relief, and now, if she was interpreting it correctly, fury. She slowly raised herself to her knees and started to back away.

Thomas was on his feet in a trice. In two quick strides he was at her side, hauling her unceremoniously to her feet.

"You're covered in mud. Let me brush you off." He ignored Sara's protests and, with one hand still closed about her upper arm like a vice, he attacked the mud clinging to the back of her jeans with somewhat more vigour than strictly necessary.

When he finally released her, Sara started to make a withering comment. After a quick glance at his expression, she swallowed it. In the face of his fury, she decided that discretion might indeed be the better part of valour. She backed away cautiously. "Uh, would you be interested in knowing what I've found?"

Thomas simply stared at her.

Ignoring his murderous expression, Sara pointed toward the sinkhole. "This sinkhole is full of fossils. There might even be an *Albertosaurus* in there."

Thomas stepped over to the opening. He lay on his stomach and attempted to look down into the cavity. She knew he couldn't see much.

"Do you have your camera with you?" he said, when he'd regained his feet. At her nod, he went to her rucksack and pulled it out.

His swift and graceful movements as he snapped pictures to aid in relocating the site reminded her of a panther stalking his prey, strength and energy restrained until he pounced.

Panthers are dangerous. I shouldn't get too close and I shouldn't provoke him. Much too easy to end up losing parts of myself to him.

Still unsmiling, Thomas broke his silence to say, "This is quite a find, Sara. I'll send out a crew first thing tomorrow morning to take a closer look."

Sara heaved a sigh of relief. She knew Thomas wasn't easily riled, but for a few minutes there, she distinctly got the impression he was reining in his temper with the thinnest of threads.

His fingers closed around her upper arm once again. "Let's go."

As they turned and headed back, she stole a glance at his face, but his expression was unreadable. What was he thinking? His touch was making her arm tingle and the feeling was starting to spread to her entire body.

They marched along in uncomfortable silence for a while. Finally Sara said, "It's always sobering to me to come across a bone bed. All that death and destruction in one place tends to make me acutely aware of my own mortality."

"Yeah, it does that."

Encouraged, Sara ventured, "So are you thinking about violence and death right now too?"

"Oh, yeah." His tone was fraught with meaning.

"The annihilation of *Albertosaurus*?"

"No."

"Then whose annihilation are you thinking about?"

Thomas's brilliant smile flickered briefly. "Yours."

They arrived back at camp just as the musicians were setting up. Several people welcomed Sara, saying, "You had us worried for a while there."

Thomas pushed her in the direction of the dining tent. "Go get something to eat. Then I want to see you in my office."

Before she went inside the dining tent, she saw Dave look at Thomas's departing back. "She's in for it now," he said, just loud enough for her to hear.

"Oh, Dave, I don't think—" Sam began.

"I know Thomas and I know that look of his." Dave slung his guitar strap over his shoulder. "It's usually directed at me."

chapter

THIRTEEN

Sara met Mike and Laura just outside the dining tent.

"We looked for you all afternoon," Laura said, "until finally Thomas found your rucksack and figured out where you were." She and Mike exchanged a glance. "We offered to help get you out, but Thomas said he'd take it from there."

Mike laughed and said, "He told us he wanted to spend a little quality time alone with you."

"Oh, did he? Well, I guess he must have enjoyed it. He's invited me to spend the evening with him too. I personally am not too sure that so much togetherness makes for a healthy relationship. I especially think that my health could suffer." Wearily, she brushed some hair out of her eyes. "If I don't turn up again in a few days, maybe you should drag the river for my remains, always assuming Thomas doesn't think drowning is too pleasant a way for me to make my way into the next dimension."

Before sitting down to eat, she apologised to everyone for having caused such a commotion in the camp. Some laughed it off; others hugged her. Everyone expressed relief that she was safe.

Everyone, that is, except Patrick, who remarked that, in his opinion, it was premature to celebrate Sara's survival before Thomas had had a go at her.

"You certainly don't appear to be overly troubled by the thought of my imminent demise." She tried to sound caustic. What was wrong with him? Wasn't he supposed to be on her side?

"One tries to be objective," Patrick said. "I'm sure you've heard the term 'survival of the fittest'. In nature, one expects to see a certain amount of natural selection taking place. Of course, one doesn't expect to see an intelligent individual self-destruct. But you shouldn't feel too bad. After all, this is not the first time that bone-headed decision-making has been responsible for the extinction of a species. History and science are both full of examples."

Patrick's rebuke stung. Dispirited, she carried her plate of food to a seat a little apart from the others. She dawdled over her supper as long as she dared. Although she had missed both breakfast and lunch, she didn't feel much like eating. Everything tasted like cardboard, and she ended up giving most of it to Barney, who, as far as anyone could tell, never ever lost his appetite.

She tuned out the noise in the tent and mulled over the events of the day. Not only was she dreading the coming inter-

Love in the Age of Dinosaurs

view with Thomas, but she was also terribly embarrassed to have caused a major disruption in the camp.

Finally, she could no longer delay going over to the field office. Before she could rise, Dave put down his guitar and came over to sit beside her. "You didn't eat much." He looked at her sympathetically. "Thomas can sometimes have that effect on people. Well, mostly on me. I can't actually recall any others losing their appetites because of him."

He pointed at Barney. "I can't tell you the number of times that that opportunistic hound has dined on fine cuisine just because Thomas has uttered the four fateful words: 'You. Over here. Now.' But I have lived to tell tales, as you can see."

He stood up and pulled her to her feet. "C'mon. You might as well get it over with. I'll walk over with you."

Barney led the way to the field office. Dave devoted the time to offering Sara some helpful hints on how to deal with an irate Thomas. "There are five simple rules that will help you to survive the ordeal before you. Rule number one is *Don't argue.* Just let him say his piece. Oh and don't look at your watch while he's doing it. That tends to make things much much worse.

"Rule number two is *Never ever, under any circumstances, say, 'yeah, yeah, I heard you the first five times'.* That is guaranteed to worsen the situation. Number three, *Never smirk.* He has a really deplorable reaction to smirking. It's sure to wipe that smile off your face for a long time to come. Rule number four: *Always apologise. And make it sound sincere.* If he thinks you're not sincere, he will make you sincerely sorry that you weren't sincere."

Dave paused to take a breath. "The fifth rule is to be used very sparingly. It cannot be guaranteed to better the situation or, I'm sorry to say, to ensure your ultimate survival. In fact, if Thomas catches you, by the time he's through with you, if you're still alive, you'll be wishing for a quick death. Nevertheless, the momentary satisfaction you get from his reaction to your words just might equal, or even outweigh, the almost certain negative outcome. If you really, really object to his tone, you can always say, *'And what would your mother say if she could hear that kind of language coming out of your mouth?'*"

Dave shook his head solemnly. "But never ever utter those words unless you have a big head start, because Tom is an awfully fast runner."

"Are you speaking from personal experience?" Sara said, with a gurgle of laughter.

Dave winced. "Actually, I only ever tried it once. It didn't end, shall we say, all that favourably, and in all honesty, I haven't been too keen for a replay."

They had reached the door to the field office. Dave said, "I don't think I'll go any farther. The unfortunate incident with the chilli peppers at lunch today hasn't quite been resolved, and I've decided that there might be something to the old adage."

"What old adage?"

"The one about absence making the heart grow fonder." Dave added earnestly, "When you go in there, just keep in mind that any suicidal feelings you have afterwards usually pass fairly quickly. And within five or six months, you probably won't even be able to recall the exact words Thomas used to put you in your place."

Sara gave Dave a hug. "Well, I guess it's 'good-bye cruel world'—"

"You'll live." He grinned and turned to leave. "And by the way, thanks!"

"For what?"

"Before you took his mind off it, I was the one scheduled for the after-dinner interview."

Sara quickly hid her smile as Thomas opened the door. He must have caught sight of Dave, because he said, "Ah. My wayward cousin. I can only imagine what kind of advice he's been giving you. Let me assure you, it will go much better for you if you disregard it."

He stood aside. "Considering the rate at which he was disappearing, I'd say that Dave has just remembered that he too has a date with me tonight."

Sara went to stand uncertainly beside the desk. Thomas closed the door and pointed to the chair in front of the desk. "Sit. You're going to be here a while." He seated himself on the other side of the desk.

"Sara—" He leaned forward and took a closer look at her shirt. "Is that blood?"

Sara looked down. She hadn't had time to change it since she and Thomas had returned to camp. It was not in very good shape. When the sun had come out earlier in the day, she had stuffed her pull-over in her rucksack, so her t-shirt bore the marks of her adventure in the sinkhole. The once-white knit was filthy, torn in several places, streaked with dark brown mud stains, and stiff with dried blood where her left arm had rested against it.

When she had washed her hands before eating, she had given her scraped arm a cursory wash, intending to do a more thorough job once she got her interview with Thomas over with. Now she became aware it was stinging quite painfully. "Oh, it's nothing," she said quickly. "Just a little scrape. I'll take care of it as soon as we're done here."

"We'll take care of it now."

Sorcha Lang

Having no choice in the matter, Sara followed him to the sink in the lab. She was very aware of him, and when he reached out and gently pulled her closer to him, her arm felt like his fingers were burning holes in it.

Thomas used a soft scrub brush and antibiotic soap to wash the scrape.

Sara couldn't help but wince. He was being quite gentle, but when the soap came into contact with the skinned area, she had to bite back a scream. "I think that's good," she hissed after a minute or so and tried to pull her arm away.

Thomas merely smiled and tightened his hold. "Oh, I don't think so, Sara. You know very well we have to get all the dirt out."

"A little dirt never hurt anyone," Sara said. "Dirt is good. Ask any worm. Now that I think of it, I'm actually quite fond of dirt. It's why I chose palaeontology. So, I really don't have a problem with leaving a little of it in there."

"A little patience goes a long way." Thomas continued to scrub. "It's how I put up with whingeing palaeontologists. The more I think about it, the fonder I am of soap. Soap is good. Ask any mother." He scrubbed a little harder.

Sara swore under her breath.

"What was that word you said?"

"Nothing," she mumbled.

"Good. I should hate to think a dirty word came out of your mouth." He continued scrubbing. "Because if it did, once I finish with the arm, I'm afraid the mouth would have to be washed out with soap."

Sara gritted her teeth, and allowed murderous thoughts to fill her mind while Thomas finished his ministrations. He chatted amicably all the while about the various types and properties of soap. By the time he had applied-antibiotic ointment and was wrapping a bandage around her arm, she had settled on strangulation as her method of choice.

"There! A job well done. Now where were we?" He led her back into the office, where he settled her none too gently on the chair in front of the desk.

Instead of going around, he leaned against the front edge, looking thoughtfully down at Sara. "You know, Sara," he began in a conversational tone, "I've had the opinion for some time now that you're sadly in need of someone to take you in hand and protect you from yourself."

It took an effort, but Sara sat quite still and quiet for the entire time it took Thomas to detail all of her transgressions and his opinion of them. At one point, she was on the verge of arguing, but with Dave's warning ringing in her ears, she held her tongue. Much as she hated to admit it, she knew Thomas was justified in much of what he said. Still, she did resent some of the things he was saying.

I'd like to give you a piece of my mind, too. You're even grumpier now than you were this morning. In my opinion, you're sadly in need of someone to take you in hand and tell you to stuff it. She glared up at him for a swift moment, but as Thomas's eyes narrowed, she quickly backed down.

Well, there's bravery and then there's stupidity. Dave's right. Better just to swallow the medicine now, no matter how vile it is. She forced her attention back to what Thomas was saying.

"...and so, we have two choices before us. Either you begin to take greater care—including drinking enough water, getting adequate rest, eating adequate meals, and stop driving yourself so hard, or..."

"Or what?" Sara said, wary.

"Or I revoke your authorisation to work in Dinosaur Provincial Park."

"You wouldn't!"

"Try me.

"I shouldn't like to, but I have the authority, and I'll use it if I decide that it's in your best interest that I do so. Continue on in the same manner as you have been, and you will discover I mean what I say."

Sara stared at him in dismay. She was shocked, not only that Thomas was considering such action, but also at her sudden awareness that she did not want to leave. She realised ruefully that her sense of belonging to his team was so complete that she had forgotten she had only been there for a couple of weeks and wouldn't be there that much longer. The thought of leaving filled her with such sadness that she was forced to acknowledge that he and his team had somehow penetrated the defensive layer of her reserve that usually prevented her from becoming too attached to people.

She went cold at the thought of this new vulnerability. She also couldn't believe that she was hearing the same lecture from Thomas that she had had from Andrew just a few weeks ago.

And Andrew had certainly meant what he said. If I'm not careful, I'll soon be the prime pariah of palaeontology.

Suddenly she couldn't bear to sit there another minute. "Okay. It's a deal. I'll try not to press myself so hard and I won't deliberately fall into any sinkholes or step on rattlesnakes or whatever else you decide you don't like." She stood up. "Can I go now?"

Thomas also stood. "Sure. We're done. Just keep in mind what I've said."

Love in the Age of Dinosaurs

Sara went back to the campfire and sat in front of the dying embers. A few others were sitting around chatting, but no one was playing music.

Patrick came over and joined her. "How're you doing?"

"Well," said Sara, "considering that I've just been flayed alive and then raked over hot coals, I guess you could say I'm doing okay."

Patrick laughed softly. "Just keep in mind that our earnest leader really does have your best interests at heart." He stopped to watch as Dave raced past them with Thomas in hot pursuit. "Ah, it looks like Thomas has solved the mystery of the hot chilli peppers."

Sara grinned as widely as Patrick did when Thomas put a head lock on Dave and pulled him towards the stream.

"Ow! That hurts! Ow! I'm telling Grandma!" was the last thing they heard Dave shout before a great splash drowned his voice.

Sara smiled reluctantly. "I guess I'm not the only one who has annoyed Thomas today."

"Not by a long shot. Those chilli peppers were *really* hot." Patrick gave her a quizzical look. "You probably didn't know this, but Thomas was very concerned about you. It totally distracted him from everything else. We were supposed to be working together on those funding proposals all morning, but that became a lost cause. Especially when the rain started. He kept going out to see if anyone had seen you or knew where you had gone. When you didn't turn up at lunchtime, he started sending out search parties in case you'd had an accident. I've never seen him so worried. His anger was probably proportional to his anxiety."

"Maybe," Sara acknowledged. "But I didn't ask for his concern. I didn't plan to worry anyone, and I certainly didn't plan to fall down a sinkhole, and I *definitely* didn't plan for Thomas to come and rescue me."

"Ah, well, then. You see how well everything has turned out despite your appalling lack of planning."

"I'm going to bed," she announced in an icy tone.

"Good plan."

chapter FOURTEEN

Sara woke to bright and sunny skies that held no trace of the rainclouds that had oppressed the area the previous day. Feeling much more cheerful than she had the night before, she headed to the office to receive her assignment for the week.

Thomas informed her that she would be spending the day guiding tourists on a day-hike.

At first she wondered if her assignment was a demotion. When Thomas announced that Sam would also be working with the tour, she recalled that every team member regularly led a group tour.

Her spirits lifted even more. Thomas appeared not to be harbouring a grudge, even though he'd been so angry.

Sorcha Lang

She was still feeling a little betrayed that Patrick had taken Thomas's side. Maybe by tonight we can put it all behind us. I really don't like being at odds with either of them. Maybe if I could do something really helpful it would reinstate me in their good books.

The temperature was steadily rising as Sara and Sam climbed into the bus in which a dozen tourists were already seated. Nine adults and a little girl around five or six were fanning their faces as they waited to begin their day of fossil-hunting with professional palaeontologists. Two young boys had claimed the back seat.

Sam spoke to the driver while Sara walked down the aisle with a roll of labels for the passengers' names. At the back, the boys, who looked about ten or eleven, were playing rock-paper-scissors. "Welcome. What are your names?"

The boy with straight blond hair and big grey eyes behind round eyeglasses told her that his name was Josh. The blue-eyed fellow with brown hair and chubby cheeks, said, "I'm Iain, with two i's."

"And one nose and two ears," Josh said.

Iain rolled his eyes at Sara. "But not a big mouth. That belongs to Josh."

Sara burst out laughing, as did Sam who was coming down the aisle.

"Find out who they're with," Sam whispered.

"Do you boys have a parent along with you this morning?" she said.

Josh snorted. "Nope. They couldn't come."

"Josh, they didn't say they couldn't." Iain looked at Sara and Sam. "My mum told my dad that if she didn't get a break from us soon she was going to hang herself from the nearest cottonwood."

"I thought she was going to drown herself in the Red Deer River," Josh said.

"No," said Iain, "not anymore. After she saw that cool bullsnake in the stream, she went off water in a big way."

"So you are here without adult supervision?" Sara said.

"No, I don't think so," said Iain. "You're here, aren't you?"

"And so am I."

"Hi, Tom," the two boys said in unison. There was a bit of scuffling as each one tried to be first to high-five Thomas.

"Oh, so you are already acquainted?" Sara glanced between the boys and Thomas. Her stomach flipped when Thomas turned the full force of his charming smile upon her.

"Oh, yes. We met a few days ago at the field office. I suggested that they might like to try a tour." He eyed the boys sternly for a moment. "And they promised their mother that they'd be on their best behaviour today, remember?"

"We didn't promise my mother," objected Josh. "She's in Toronto with my dad, going to a bunch of concerts and boring old museums."

"You mean to say she gave up camping with you in Dinosaur Provincial Park to go and do stuff like that?" Sara assumed a shocked expression.

"Yeah," said Josh. "She said that the last time she camped here with us, she nearly chopped us up and fed us to the rattlesnake."

"We think she was just joking," Iain said, "but she looked kind of violent when she said it."

Thomas raised an eyebrow. "What rattlesnake was she talking about?"

"Oh, the one we were trying to catch," Josh said. "We wanted to get a better look at it and—"

"Rattlesnakes?" Several other passengers repeated the word with emphasis. "You mean we're going to be seeing rattlesnakes?"

"You might well see a rattlesnake," Thomas said as he led Sara and Sam back to the front of the bus. "You will almost certainly be seen by one. They are generally not a problem. A snake will only bite if it feels threatened. The important thing is to stay with the group and not go wandering off alone." He eyed Sara for a split second before directing a stern gaze at Josh and Iain. "And *never* attempt to capture a rattlesnake. We treat rattlesnakes with total respect and we leave them alone. Are we clear about that?"

All the adults fervently agreed. The disappointed look Josh and Iain exchanged suggested that they had expected much greater things of Thomas.

"What do we do if we see one?" a woman said.

"The important thing is to locate the snake," replied Thomas. "A snake will often rattle as, or after, you walk by it. The instinct is to step back—right onto the snake's head. In the unlikely event you hear a snake rattle at you, don't panic. Stop and figure out where it is. Then you can move away from it."

"Oh, okay, sure," said the woman faintly.

"You'll be fine." Thomas smiled. "Now, if Sara will start the air-conditioning, we'll do the One-Finger Oath and then we can be off."

Sara walked down the aisle again, this time misting everyone with water from a spray bottle. The passengers began to laugh, but then they turned their attention to Thomas, who was telling them to raise their right index fingers so that they could recite the oath. There was a bit of a delay while Josh figured out which was the middle and which the index finger. Thomas levelled a look at him and started heading in his direction to lend assistance. He quickly solved the puzzle.

"That's better," said Thomas. "Now, repeat after me: I solemnly swear…that I will use one finger…and one finger only…to touch rocks and fossils…and that I will not move…or break or harm or collect…any natural resource. Nor will I…join my one finger…to the finger of anyone else…to move or collect…any natural resource."

Once the bus was underway, Sam began to explain why Dinosaur Provincial Park had been designated a World Heritage Site. "There are three reasons. The first is the riparian—or riverside—habitat alongside the Red Deer River. The extensive cottonwoods growing by the water provide a home for 165 different species of birds. Does anyone know what special adaptive feature these trees have for survival in dry conditions?"

Iain, who was attempting to throw Josh's hat to the front of the bus, while fending off Josh, who was trying equally hard to prevent it, paused for a moment to say, "If the year is too dry, the cottonwood can shut off nutrients to its branches, and then in better, moister years, it can open up the flow of water again. So bare branches in the summer don't mean that the tree is dead." The hat sailed through the air and was caught by Thomas, who had relocated himself to the back of the bus.

"That's correct," said Sam, coughing slightly. "Very good, Iain."

"The second reason for World Heritage Site status," said Josh, in a nasal, pedantic tone, "is because of the barren hills and ridges that make up the badlands. The name 'badlands' comes from the French term *'mauvaises terres à traverser'*, which was what some snooty French traders called Montana and the Dakotas because they didn't think the land was good for livestock grazing or farming. They didn't know *anything* about dinosaurs."

"Uh, that's right, Josh." Sam sounded bemused. "Does anyone have anything to add?"

Iain picked himself up from the floor where he had landed when Josh pushed him out of their seat. Thomas plunked him into an empty seat and seated himself between the two boys.

As if he'd been sitting quietly the whole time, Iain said, "The Badlands' rate of deterioration is very rapid. This state of erosion occurs primarily during spring runoff, causing tiny rills to form on the surface of hills and valleys. Given time, the rills will enlarge to create countless gullies, sugar loafs, ravines, coulees, jagged divides, and ultimately canyons. Surface rain water, known as sheetwash, carries clay and sediment debris away rapidly. Evidence of dendritic—that means branching—channels or rillwash are seen all over the park. This is why vegetation is almost totally absent, as showers wash away material before plants can gain a foothold."

He paused for a breath. "Piping refers to the subsurface removal of sand and silt particles via the action of running water, which leaves behind a network of interconnecting underground voids and tunnels that collapse with time, forming gullies. Sinkholes are a result of gulley heads formed by widened pipings which collapse to form crater-like surfaces."

Everyone but the driver turned to stare at the two boys.

Sara exchanged a look with Thomas and laughed. "I gather you have read Gordon Reid's book, *Dinosaur Provincial Park*. Do you have a photographic memory? Maybe we should call you 'Encyclopedia Brown', after that fictional boy detective."

"That's not what his mum calls him," Josh said with a smirk. "She calls him Irritator One after that real irritating fossil from Brazil."

"I wouldn't talk if I were you, since she calls you Irritator Two." He turned to Sara. "It's sort of like Thing One and Thing Two from Dr. Seuss, only with a dinosaur twist. She's a librarian. And she likes dinosaurs. And she thinks she's funny."

The boys rolled their eyes and said together, "But she's not!"

"Well," said Sam, when she had recovered, although her voice was still a little shaky with laughter, "that brings us to the third reason that Dinosaur Provincial Park is a World Heritage Site. And that reason is—"

"Fossils!" everyone said, happy to at last contribute to the conversation.

"That's correct," Sara said as the bus came to a stop. "And our first stop is to look at some of those very special fossils. Please follow me."

Josh and Iain immediately began to sing "Follow Me".

Many of the adults and all three of the palaeontologists joined in singing the familiar tune. The second time through the chorus, Thomas smiled and took Sara's hand as they sang the last line.

At his touch, she felt a jolt somewhere deep inside and her body began to tingle the way it had the day before. Her heart began to beat a little faster. They locked eyes and for a split second she had a strange sensation of drowning in Thomas's blue depths.

Thomas squeezed her hand gently and laughed as the song ended. Sara laughed with him, but just as they let go, a look of ineffable sadness crossed her face. It was gone so quickly that he almost doubted that he had seen it.

Sara's usual broad smile was in place as they crowded around the fossil bed. "It's been quite a while since I've heard anyone singing John Denver," Sara said as they were walking to the fossil bed. "My—Josh and Iain are quite a pair. Is that why you decided to come along with us this morning? I have a feeling we're going to be awfully glad you're here before the day is over."

Thomas heard the slight hesitation before Sara started talking about the boys. He was positive she had been about to say something else, and he wondered what it was. Nevertheless, he grinned and said, "Oh, have you gotten over your initial disappointment?"

Sara reddened when he leaned forward and tucked a lock of hair behind her ear. He said softly, "Don't think I didn't notice that expression on your face when you discovered I was along for the ride. Were you hoping to spend the day alone with Sam?"

"Don't be silly!" she retorted. "We'd better get started before the boys start entertaining themselves."

Thomas shouted, "Beware of jelly mud!"

At that exact moment Josh cried out with glee, "Hey! Jelly mud!"

Thomas moved fast, but was only just in time to prevent the little girl from joining the boys in the shallow puddle, where they were happily arguing over who was most stuck.

He groaned. "Jelly mud," he explained to the adult onlookers, "occurs because of the bentonitic clay which comprises the soil here. We had rain yesterday, which moistened the dirt, creating this slick goo, which is capable of sucking one's shoes off. As you can see."

While Thomas assisted the boys, Sam grinned wickedly and said, "So Sara, I hope you're noticing how good Thomas is with children. That's important information you'll want to file away for future use."

Sara felt her face grow warm, but she raised her brows and replied sweetly, "Oh, absolutely, I'm noticing. But why should I file it away? I can use it now. Let me assure you he'll make a very good father to your children."

Sam's smile grew wider. "They'll be gorgeous, you know—yours and Thomas's. I'm so looking forward to seeing them."

"Well, as there is absolutely no likelihood of their future existence, I'm afraid you'd better start accepting the fact that you won't be seeing them. Ever. Sorry to disappoint, but there it is." She put her arm around Sam and said consolingly, "Just give yourself some time. When you have enough real children of your own, I'm sure you'll forget all about any imaginary ones of mine."

She doesn't think I mean it, But the last thing on earth I want to have is a husband and a family. Better not to have at all than to have and then to lose.

"There, now! Don't do that again."

Thomas had one hand on each of the boys' shoulders. They were grinning broadly and trying unsuccessfully to punch each other behind Thomas's back as they rejoined the group.

But she's right about Thomas. If they look like him, his children will be gorgeous. And smart. And lively. Probably quite a bit like Josh and Iain, but I won't be around to see them.

With a pang, Sara realised she wouldn't be a part of Thomas's future. Once the summer was over, their paths might never cross again. Caught off guard by her distress at that reality, she hastily thrust her attention in other directions. A curious throbbing remained, as if she had been fencing with her thoughts and had parried too late to prevent a painful nick.

Pasting a smile on her face, she led the group over to a *Centrosaurus* bone bed and began to explain the exhibit. "As you can see, there are no fully articulated specimens in this bed. We say a skeleton is articulated when it is found in one piece, with the bones still attached in the proper order. But that is not the case here. It's all a mixed-up jumble. There are several complete skeletons here, but we have no way of knowing which bones belong to which skeletons."

"So what happened here?" asked the man with "Ray" written on his nametag.

"Well, one explanation could be that they died of some sort of disease," Sara said.

"Aw, that's so lame," Josh scoffed. "Wasn't there any carnage?"

"Yeah. We thrive on carnage," Iain said. "Tell us something about carnage."

"A second, carnage-filled explanation, is that a migrating herd of *Centrosaurs* was trying to ford a river. They were probably good swimmers, and some of the herd might have made it to the other side. However, in the rushing floodwaters after a storm, the river would have been very high and the current very strong. Perhaps some of the dinosaurs lost their footing or were knocked over. There would have been a lot of jostling and stumbling, and in the end, they would have dragged each other down to a watery death. Their carcasses would have drifted downstream and come to rest on sandbars or banks of the river.

"Once they were aware dinner was being served, the carnivores would have arrived with big appetites and sharp eating utensils—teeth. They dug in, shall we say, with gusto, leaving behind tooth marks, some of their own teeth, broken bones, that kind of thing. After that, the corpses would have been buried quickly by sediment. The soft tissue would have decomposed, but the hard parts gradually fossilised by absorbing calcium, silica and carbon."

"That's more like it," Josh said, sounding satisfied.

Love in the Age of Dinosaurs

When the group was once more seated in the bus, they drove to an isolated area to begin their fossil-hunting. Everyone sat in a circle on the ground while Thomas took out a box of fossils and began to explain how to identify a fossil. "First," he said, "we check the rock for striations. Fossils, like wood, have lines running through them. Next, check its weight. If it has striations, but is too light to be a rock, then it's a piece of wood. However, if it passes the first two tests, it's time for the lick test."

"The lick test?" repeated the woman named Rhonda. "You mean with our tongues?"

"Yes. We lick the sample. If it's a fossil, it'll stick to your tongue. Tiny pores in the bone create suction and that's why it sticks."

"To my tongue?"

"Well, you could lick your finger and press hard to see if it sticks."

"It's way cooler to use your tongue." Josh happily popped a piece of rock into his mouth. Then he made a face. "Yuck. Is that what a fossil tastes like?"

"Probably not," Thomas said, "since what you are sucking on is mudstone. If the rock is dark, it's mudstone; fossils are lighter in colour."

The group milled about, searching in the same general area, for the next couple of hours. Shortly before noon, Sara and Thomas, who were momentarily isolated from the others by a hoodoo, spotted a bone at the same instant. They both reached for it and their fingers became entangled.

His hand closed around hers. He held it lightly for a few seconds, softy caressing it with his thumb. Sara remained immobile while Thomas mesmerised her with his look and his gentle touch. He moved his head forward until their lips were almost touching. Suddenly he let go and swept up the fossil with his free hand. "Mine!" He held it up triumphantly.

"You big cheater!"

"All's fair in love and war." Thomas was grinning widely.

"Is this war?" Sara couldn't help asking.

"No, I don't think so." He smiled again, but a strange expression crossed his face. Before she could ask if anything was wrong, Sam announced that it was time for lunch, and that they would be eating in a special place.

"Are we going to eat inside an *Iguanodon*?" Iain said.

"No," said Thomas, "but we have somewhere that's almost as good. Have you ever been to Egypt?"

They boarded the bus once again and it wound its way through the area named the Valley of the Castles. They stopped near a couple of hoodoos that did look as if they belonged in Egypt. One looked like a camel, and the other resembled a pyramid.

Sam and Sara handed out lunch bags and drinks as everyone got off the bus. On the way to the picnic area, Thomas loosely encircled Sara's shoulders with one arm. "Did you keep a bottle of water for yourself?"

"I did."

"Good. All that talking tends to dehydrate a person." He squeezed her shoulder briefly. "By the way, you're doing a great job."

Surprised at the compliment, Sara felt pleasure suffuse her entire body. She started to thank him, but he turned away as someone called his name.

Thomas seated himself close beside Sara.

Josh suddenly said, "Hey, anybody know some good jokes?"

"Yes!" shouted Iain.

Love in the Age of Dinosaurs

"Okay," said Josh. "Iain's going first."

"When do birds evolve?" asked Iain.

No one knew.

"When the dino soars!" he shouted.

"Which dinosaurs were the most polite?" Josh said.

When no one came up with an answer, he chortled. "The *plesiosaurs*!"

Sara had to laugh. "Are you boys making these jokes up on the spot?"

"'Course," said Iain. "All the written-down jokes are really lame. Why don't you try?"

"Okay," said Sara. "Where does the mother send the young dinosaur when he's naughty?"

Both boys shook their heads, admitting defeat.

"To the Badlands."

A few adults chuckled.

Josh and Iain exchanged a look. "Keep trying," said Iain. "I'm sure you'll get the hang of it."

"I've got one," said Thomas. "Which horned dinosaur was the first to use a camera?"

Again no one had a good answer.

"Photoceratops."

Josh and Iain shouted with laughter. "Good one!" Iain gave him a high five.

The dinosaur jokes went on for some time. Some of the adults even contributed. Eventually Thomas suggested they continue their tour.

"That was fun!" Patricia's mother said as they re-boarded the bus.

"Most of you were very good at it," Iain said. "And those who weren't might still improve with a lot of practice." He looked pointedly at Sara.

Thomas watched Sara laughingly tousle Iain's hair and then crouch down to show Patricia something on the ground. She put her arm around the little girl, and Patricia immediately wrapped her own arms around Sara's neck and hugged her. He reluctantly dragged his eyes away when Sam addressed him.

"She's good with kids," Sam said. "Maybe someday she'll have some of her own to hug and cuddle."

"Hmm," Thomas responded. He could well imagine Sara all wrapped up in a warm physical embrace, but the picture in his mind was not at all maternal. And it wasn't filled with children.

Sam continued to chat. "I think Sara's children will be very smart and very lively."

"And probably very prone to getting themselves into hot water," Thomas added drily.

"And definitely very pretty," Sam said.

"That too," agreed Thomas.

Several hours later, the palaeontologists arrived back at the dining tent. Thomas was carting everything but some wild roses that Sara had stuck in a water bottle. His gift, which she had insisted on carrying herself.

"Well, Thomas," said Sam, surveying the spread before them, "you were right. It is steakosaurus tonight."

"Is there a story here, Tom?" inquired Patrick curiously as he filled a plate. "Sara and Sam look done-in. I thought you were just doing the tour group today."

"The tour group and then some," groaned Sara.

They all took their full plates outside and sat on the benches arranged around the campfire. Dave neatly squeezed in beside Sara.

"We had a couple of somewhat lively ten-year-olds on the tour today." With one well-directed push, Thomas upended Dave and seated himself beside Sara.

Dave jumped back up, as if intending to retaliate, but Patrick reached out a strong arm and yanked Dave down beside him. Dave glared at Patrick and muttered something extremely rude, but Patrick didn't shift his gaze, even when he delivered a stinging cuff that left Dave wincing.

Both Sam and Sara were regarding Thomas disbelievingly.

"*Somewhat lively?*" Sam said.

Sara added, "An exploding hydrogen bomb has less energy than those two kids."

"What two kids?" asked Barry, who had just joined them, balancing a heaping plate in one hand and holding a frothy drink in the other.

"Thomas invited two somewhat lively ten-year-old boys to come on the tour today. I don't know what we'd have done if Thomas hadn't taken pity on us and come along to help supervise them," Sam explained.

Thomas described everything that had happened that day.

The other palaeontologists looked a little shell-shocked. "Well, did you at least sign them up for next year's field season?" Patrick finally asked.

Sara suddenly stood and said that she had to go to bed. Thomas just as suddenly stood and said that he had a number of things to do in the office.

Before he could leave, Sam said, "Thomas, you *did* ask them if they were available next year for the volunteer programme."

"And?" prompted Patrick.

"And, that was really funny, because then Josh asked if Tom and Sara would be back from their honeymoon and out here by then." She sent a roguish glance in Thomas's direction. If he hadn't been afraid of being thought a coward, he would have headed for his office.

"I guess Tom wasn't really listening to the question because he sort of absent-mindedly said 'oh, yeah, of course' at the same time that Sara indignantly snapped 'certainly not'. And then Iain said disgustedly, 'Geez, Josh. Why'd you have to go and ask something dumb like that? It's obvious that they're not getting married...You can tell from the way they disagree that they already are.

"And then he turned to Tom and said, 'So, I guess we can come.'"

Unable to think of a suitable rejoinder, Thomas stomped off to his office.

chapter

FIFTEEN

The next several days passed in a blur. Twice more Thomas scheduled himself to go on group tours with Sara, requiring them to spend long days together. Each day was filled with laughter and fun, which more than compensated for the good-natured teasing that came their way.

No one ever said anything directly, but Sara sometimes wondered if people were deliberately clearing the way for a romance between her and Thomas. There always seemed to be an empty seat beside her for Thomas to slide into, and even Dave melted into the scenery when Thomas sought her out.

Sara was content to let things continue as they were because she continually reassured herself that she and Thomas were not a couple. She absolutely did not want to get seriously involved with anyone, and she planned to call a halt to anything with Thomas long before things became at all serious. She was in complete control of the situation, although she did sometimes have the niggling feeling that someone was going to get burnt if she kept on playing with fire.

Thomas and I are just good friends, like Patrick and me...Well, okay, maybe not quite like Patrick and me. But it's not a romantic relationship. Because if it were, Thomas would kiss me. Or at least try to. And he never does. I wonder why. No, scratch that. I don't care why, because I don't want him to kiss me. I just want to be friends, nothing more. And that's what we are.

We enjoy each other's company, we laugh a lot together, we have common interests and values, and we can talk to one another. And Thomas doesn't talk to everyone. Usually he just listens. He rarely says anything about himself. But he's starting to tell me things about himself. That must mean that he trusts me and feels he can confide in me.

So maybe a friendship with me is just what Thomas needs right now. And that's all it is—friendship. We're not taking it in any other direction. It's perfectly natural for people who are just friends to notice how insanely good-looking their friends are. I wonder why he's never kissed me.

Thomas did begin to open up and share some details of his personal life with her. Quite often the stories he told her of his training and fieldwork and his family history with Dave had her doubled over with laughter. The more time Sara spent with him, the more she enjoyed his company.

The evening of their final tour together he mentioned that he was leaving the next day for the Therapod Symposium and would be gone for a week.

"I thought the symposium was only for three days," Sara said. She was sitting between Patrick and Thomas at the campfire, and idly throwing a stick for Barney to fetch.

"It is, but there are some other things I have to do while I'm there. Patrick will be joining me for meetings with government officials regarding a tract of land southeast of the current park boundaries. It's Crown land that is currently up for grabs. We're sure it is prime fossil-bearing land. We're lobbying hard to convince the government to extend the current boundaries of the park to encompass the area. We have a lot of support from educational institutions and palaeontology societies and the general public.

"Unfortunately, however, we are not the only stakeholders. A consortium of powerful and wealthy businessmen is interested in developing the site for tourism. They are proposing some huge development, with numerous hotels, casinos, you name it."

"Why don't you give the government bigwigs a tour of the area? Show them what's there?" Sara said.

"We plan to, once we can get out there and do some serious prospecting. But, as you know, we've had a difficult field season and we haven't had a chance. Weather problems and personnel shortages have played havoc with our plans." Thomas's frustration was evident in his tone. "We haven't had the funds or the people to pursue this the way I'd like. That's why we've been spending so much time on that PAIN application. If we are successful in obtaining funding from PAIN, we can dedicate those dollars to the park boundary issue."

Patrick said, "It would help from a public relations perspective if we had something really special to show the world." He looked skyward and said, "Where's the big discovery when we need it? You know the kind I'm talking about, the one that somehow captures the public imagination and has the phones ringing off the hook. The ensuing media coverage would add more pressure on the government to preserve the lands."

Thomas laughed. "Yeah, well, if wishes were horses...The farmers around here all say, 'This is next year country'. I guess that holds true for palaeontologists too." He stood. "I'll see you two tomorrow. I have a few more things to do before I leave."

"Patrick," said Sara, after Thomas had gone. "I'd really like to help with that PAIN application. I'm sure you're eligible for extra funding and I know I can help you to get it."

Patrick shook his head. "I know you'd like to help, Sara, and I don't doubt your sincerity. But when you mentioned the discretionary funds category before, I called PAIN and talked to them about it. I was categorically told that we were not eligible and not to bother applying. In fact, they warned me that some groups have been padding their projected expenses, so PAIN's response has been to reduce the amounts awarded.

"If I apply for extra funds, PAIN might interpret it as padding my expenses and they might well end up reducing the amount they allocate to us. I simply can't afford to risk it. We really need every cent we've requested and I don't want to do anything to jeopardise our chances of getting it."

"Who did you talk to?" Sara said. "Aaron or Jay? They're the ones who actually know what's going on."

Patrick paused to think. "I can't remember who told me we weren't eligible. Somebody I didn't know. But then I think I spoke to Adrian...yeah, it was Adrian. And he warned me about the problem with people padding their expenses."

"Adrian!" Sara scowled and didn't bother hiding her scorn. "I'm so sick of people telling me what Adrian thinks. Adrian doesn't think. He never knows anything. He just talks like he knows. That just proves you should listen to me."

"Sorry, Sara, but I just can't risk it."

Sara fumed as Patrick walked away. In frustration, she hurled Barney's stick into the fire, an action she immediately regretted when Barney hung his head and tail and looked at her reproachfully. "Sorry, Barney. What can I do to make it up to you?"

Barney wagged his tail and headed for the path along the stream. He stopped after a few metres, cocked his head, and looked at her expectantly.

Okay, Sara told herself, as she followed Barney down the trail. *Watch the dog and learn. Do not hold a grudge. Do not hold a grudge. Do not hold a...*

The next morning Sara, Dave and Patrick were receiving Thomas's final instructions for the week ahead when Thomas suddenly glanced at his watch and yelped, "Look, I've got to get going. I have to stop at the museum to drop off the mail and some other papers before I head into Calgary. Time is really getting tight."

He gathered up some loose sheets and folders. At the door he paused and turned around. "You know, Patrick, I might as well take the PAIN application with me now. It's completed; no use having it hang around here getting lost under other piles of paper." He returned to the desk and started rifling through various documents that covered the surface.

Dave suddenly stiffened.

"What's wrong, Dave? Are you okay?" Thomas said.

Dave rolled his shoulders. "Yeah, fine. I just got a funny kind of spasm in my back, but it's gone now."

Thomas continued to sift through the papers on the desk. "Where'd it go? I could have sworn I saw it here earlier."

Patrick frowned. "Maybe it's still in my tent. Hang on, I'll just go and check. Back in a sec." He left at a run.

Sara grabbed Dave's arm and pushed him in the direction of the room that housed the photocopier. "We'll check the supply room, Tom," she called. "Maybe you should check your tent, too."

"I'm pretty sure it's not there, but I guess it doesn't hurt to check again. Be right back."

Sara watched from the doorway as he left the office. "Good! We have a couple of minutes. Give it to me."

Dave pulled the application out from under his shirt with a flourish. "Ta Da!" He whistled admiringly, "Wow, Sara, I've always said that palaeontology is a dead end for you. Have you ever considered a career as a pickpocket? That was the fastest sleight of hand I've seen since I saw *Oliver Twist* at the Stratford Festival. What are we stealing? Will it make us lots of money? Are you planning a long life of looting and plundering for us? Or will we just run away together and live happily ever after at Thomas's expense?"

Sara felt a twinge of shame, but she grinned. "We're not stealing anything, you wretch. I just need to get a look at this application before it goes out. Patrick and I don't see eye to eye on this. Since he's wrong and I'm right, I have to do what I have to do."

Dave raised an eyebrow in imitation of Thomas and adopted a stern tone, "And what exactly is it that you have to do, young lady?"

"Just hand me that pen over there, and keep your mouth shut and your eyes open while I fix this. Don't let anyone in this room."

"Your every wish is my command." Dave obediently went to the supply room door and blocked the entrance.

Sara started writing furiously on the application forms. She was filling in the last blank when she heard the door open. "Sara?" Patrick called. "Did you find it? Thomas is waiting in the Jeep."

Dave quickly answered. "Yeah, we found it. We're just photocopying it. Tell Tom he'll have it in a couple of minutes."

"Don't you dare tell anyone about this," Sara whispered as she started copying.

Dave gave her a wounded look and pretended he'd been stabbed in the heart. "Me? Tell? After what I've been through for you? I never did tell Thomas who smuggled in those chilli peppers, you know. I endured physical torture, and a dunking in cold water, not to mention a mind-numbing lecture, and still my lips were sealed."

"You really are a wretch." Sara had to laugh. "If I had known what you were going to do with them, I never would have gotten them for you."

"How did you get them anyway? I've been wondering."

"Ben Stowe passed by one morning and said he'd be coming through again in the afternoon. I just gave him your list."

Sara placed the application forms in a brown envelope and labelled it. She patted him gently on the cheek as they walked out to the Jeep. "Thanks. And just remember, you had no idea what I was up to. All you did was hold onto some papers for me."

chapter

SIXTEEN

Thomas drained his glass and concluded his story about the symposium. "So, although we agreed on nothing else, at least we were all agreed that the fossil was a dinosaur."

Mary and Patrick laughed. They were seated at Mary and Patrick's kitchen table in Calgary, having a quick visit before Patrick and Thomas returned to Dinosaur Provincial Park. "So now what is the priority for the rest of the season?" Mary said. "You only have a couple of weeks left."

"Prospecting, mostly," Thomas said. "That's if the weather holds. We'll continue with the work of locating old quarries, and I'd like to send a few people outside the park into that southeast section we've been coveting."

"I wish I could be there," sighed Mary. "If it weren't for the anaemia, I'd have enough energy to go out prospecting." She grimaced. "Not that I can bend that far forward anymore. And when I'm erect, I can't even see my feet these days. But for you, Thomas, I'd bend over backwards if I could."

"That's okay." Thomas had to smile. "We need you to have a healthy delivery more than we need you to be out hunting for dinosaurs."

"More lemonade?" Mary started to get up, but Patrick pushed her back into her chair. "I'll get it, Mary. Just sit." He topped up the three glasses of lemonade.

"So, speaking of Sara," Mary hinted.

"Were we?" Thomas raised an eyebrow.

Mary grinned. "Well, why don't we? How is she?"

"How is Sara?" Thomas repeated. "Well, Sara is a fine palaeontologist. Dedicated, perceptive, precise, hardworking. She is a great team-player and also works well individually. She's popular with the others on the team, Dave and Barney love her, and the tourists seem to really like her too."

"And you really like her too, right?" she said.

Thomas caught Patrick bestowing a laughing glance upon his wife as he gently squeezed Mary's arm.

"Of course I like her. A lot, in fact," Thomas assured her.

"How much is 'a lot'?"

"A lot more than most," Thomas admitted, "but..."

"But?" said Mary.

Thomas shrugged. "I have some doubts."

"Doubts? About Sara?" Mary appeared genuinely shocked. Her voice got a little louder. "What could you possibly doubt about Sara? She's a brilliant palaeontologist, a tried and true friend, and an outstanding human being." She exhaled sharply as she started to laugh. "Oh, stop it. I'm not going to shoot you."

Thomas, who had leaned sideways out of the line of fire, raised his arms in surrender. He cautiously lowered them a bit, and asked Patrick, "Is it safe to come out?"

Patrick gave Mary a one-armed hug. "Mary is Sara's biggest fan. Even though I've known Sara longer, Mary is, in some ways, closer to her. Something to do with being women, I guess."

"Sara's as close to you as she is to me. It's just that sometimes you get on your high horse and start bossing her around. Or try to. She knows she can count on me to re-inflate her ego after you've flattened her with one of your lectures."

"You mean to say that I actually get through to her once in a while?" Patrick said in mock surprise. "Well, hallelujah! There's hope after all."

"Oh, stop it," Mary protested. "You're too hard on her sometimes. You seem to forget what she's been through."

"No, Mary." Patrick's voice had gone soft. "I don't forget anything. It's Sara who forgets. Forgets how to live, how to find joy, how to look after herself."

Mary's fine dark eyes were troubled. "So is she..."

"She's the same," Patrick said.

"Oh, no! I was so sure that if we got her back here this summer..."

"Let's back up a minute here," said Thomas. "Are you telling me that the two of you are also concerned about Sara's health?"

"Big time. We have been for a long while." Patrick ran his fingers through his hair. "I know you are too, and you've only known her for a few weeks."

Thomas nodded in agreement. "I've spoken to her a few times about proper safety precautions in the field and getting enough rest and nourishment. One minute, she agrees to take more care, and then the next minute she's doing exactly the same things she promised not to do."

Mary frowned. "For example?"

"For example," said Thomas, "she is obviously totally exhausted, yet she is always the first one up and the last to leave the field. I told her to take a day off while I'm away, but there is absolutely no doubt in my mind that she did not follow my instructions." He let his voice express his frustration. "I shudder to think how many old quarries and new specimens she's found in the last week. We'll probably have to extend the field season by a month to deal with it all."

"Well, that's something in her favour." Mary chuckled. "There's no denying she has a gift for discovery."

"Sara throws herself into her work with such mindless abandon that I sometimes think she's in danger of losing herself completely." Thomas hesitated, and then added slowly, "And I don't think she's happy. She puts on a good face for the public. She seems to be enjoying herself, and she laughs as much as, or more than, anyone else. But I've noticed an undercurrent of sadness flowing pretty strongly beneath that unruffled surface. She never speaks of it, but it's there, in her eyes, when she thinks no one is looking."

"Sara is profoundly grief-stricken," agreed Patrick. "It has never been properly resolved, and it's eating away at her. So she throws herself into her work, which is draining her dry. She continuously drives herself and I don't think she either eats or sleeps enough. That's why she's so thin and exhausted-looking."

Love in the Age of Dinosaurs

Mary rubbed her forehead. "It's her recklessness that troubles me. Sara never used to be like that. Before the accident, she took normal precautions, and behaved very sensibly. Afterwards she changed, and personal safety was just no longer a priority. Over the last few years, we've heard some real horror stories from Andrew Turner about the chances she's taken and the scrapes she's gotten into."

"I've read her the riot act a number of times," Patrick said, "and so has Andrew. She always promises to take more care, but I think deep down, she feels she has nothing left to lose. Not that she has a death wish or anything. It's more that she just doesn't see the point of worrying too much about her health or safety. After all, common sense didn't protect her family."

Thomas said, "Well, how did it get to this point? Didn't anyone suggest grief counselling? Weren't there any relatives to step in and offer support?"

Mary sighed. "People have done what they could. There aren't any relatives to speak of. Well, there might be a second cousin or something in England, but there's no one here at all. There was just the nuclear family—mum, dad, Sara, and Alex. There were friends of course—friends of Sara's parents, and Sara's friends—but that's not the same. And we were all so young. And stupid. We didn't know what to do."

Patrick added, "And of course, Sara herself is very stubborn and hasn't necessarily listened to whatever advice we've given, good or bad. She's just determined to bury it all inside and carry on as usual."

"I think perhaps it's less stubbornness than simple self-preservation." Mary sounded thoughtful. "She just doesn't want to be overwhelmed by grief. She told me once that if ever she did begin to cry, she knew she would never ever stop. And so she has never allowed herself to start."

"She never broke down? Not even at the funeral?"

"No," Patrick and Mary said in unison.

"Especially not then," Mary said. "You should have seen her at the memorial service. We all thought she should allow others to take over and at least help plan the readings and the music, but Sara wouldn't have it. She said it was one last thing she could do for those she loved."

Patrick took up the tale. "But although she chose them, she did let me and Dr. Byrne, an old family friend, do the readings. She hired a string quartet for the music. She had some connections because the family was involved in the local music scene."

"But then at the end of the service, Sara and her trio played tributes for each of them." Mary said. "And Patrick sang."

"I didn't know Sara played any instruments," Thomas said. "She has never mentioned it."

"Oh, she plays," Patrick assured him. "Or did. She hasn't picked up an instrument since the funeral. Alex was known as the talented one, but the whole family played. Sara played flute and piano, sometimes a little guitar. She always said she wasn't that musical, but the rest of us thought she did all right."

"And she was in a trio?"

"Yes," said Mary. "There were three women—Maura on harp, Sara on flute, Joan on piano. They were good."

"What did they play?" asked Thomas.

Patrick shrugged. "Different sorts of music. Some classical. Some folk. Some pop. At the funeral, they played three songs for Sara's mother, father, and brother. And then as people filed out, they played 'Ashokan Farewell'."

Love in the Age of Dinosaurs

"I had never heard them play so well. And as soon as the last note died out, Sara put her flute in its case and gave the case away."

"Pretty much like her whole life," said Patrick. "She sold or donated almost everything she owned, and now she avoids anything that reminds her of the past. She doesn't even behave the way she used to."

"So," said Mary after a short silence. She drummed her fingers on the table.

"So...what?" Patrick gave her a suspicious look.

"So we need to put our heads together and decide how we're going to help Sara through this." Mary nodded decisively. "Thomas, what is your solution?"

Thomas jumped. "My solution? I don't have a solution. I didn't have one before, I don't have one now, and I certainly don't expect to have a solution in the future. I think the best plan is to consult a specialist in grief therapy."

"Oh, we've already done that," Mary waved her hand dismissively. "He was useless. Dr. Byrne, who has known Sara all her life, said that in his opinion Sara was quite correct in thinking that she needed time and distance to deal with such a devastating event. It was probably good that she left for a while. But last spring, when I told him I thought Sara was pining away, he said it was probably time to get her to come back. Which, I can assure you, was no mean feat. Now that she's here, he says we need to get her to talk about it."

"How are you going to do that? She doesn't ever talk about her family. She sometimes starts to say something, and then she quickly changes the topic. Did I say something funny?" Thomas demanded, as Mary and Patrick began to smile.

Mary got up and gave him a hug. "Not funny, no, but that's just about the most fantastic thing you've ever said."

Thomas directed a puzzled look first at Mary, and then at Patrick, who was also nodding in a satisfied way. "I'm not sure we're exactly on the same wavelength here."

"It's like this," Patrick said. "Dr. Byrne said if Sara began to mention her family, subconsciously at least she's ready to take the next step. I've been around Sara for weeks, and she's never mentioned them at all. Nor has she said anything to Mary."

"So you know what that means." Mary sounded excited.

Thomas shook his head. "Well, no, actually, I don't think I do."

"That means you're the logical person to get her to talk."

"Me? Oh, no, I don't think so. I care a lot about Sara and I would love to help her," Thomas said, "but I'm not at all comfortable choosing to do something that could go so very, very wrong."

"Is that all that's worrying you?" Patrick said. "It's not a choice you would feel comfortable making?"

Thomas nodded.

"Well then, mate, your worries are over!" Patrick punched him lightly on the arm. "You don't have to make that choice at all."

"Good." Thomas heaved a sigh of relief.

"Because it appears Sara has already chosen for you."

"And now all you have to do to demonstrate your love and concern for Sara," Mary concluded, "is to be mean enough to make her cry."

chapter

SEVENTEEN

Thomas stared blindly out the window, barely registering the blur of telephone poles as they whizzed by. He thought it was a good thing that Patrick was driving them back to the site, because he was incapable of focussing on the road. Mary's last words were still ringing in his head, and he had spent the entire ride silently replaying the whole conversation that had taken place.

He kept coming to the same conclusion. Mary and Patrick were mistaken. Much as he would like to help Sara, he was simply not qualified to do so. If he barrelled his way into her private woes, he could end up making things very much worse. Where would they be then?

There was no way he felt comfortable taking on that kind of responsibility. Especially for someone he'd only known for a few short years...

Wait a minute. I'm really losing it here. I've only known Sara a few weeks. I guess it just feels like years because of that discussion about Sara's past. I've known Mary and Patrick for years, and they've known Sara for years, and so I feel that I've known her for years too.

"Just in time for supper." Patrick's announcement interrupted Thomas's reverie. "I wonder what Dave's serving up tonight. I'm starving."

With an effort, Thomas pulled his thoughts back to the present. He unfastened his seat belt. "It smells like a barbecue. Let's go."

He dumped his gear inside his tent and headed for the dining tent. Several people called greetings.

"Tom! Pat! Help yourselves to a burger. There are still some on the barbecue." Rob gestured with a beer stein.

Thomas looked around curiously. "Where's Dave?"

Geoff opened a bag of buns. "Oh, he and Sara aren't back yet. So we started without them."

"Dave and Sara? Where'd they go?" Thomas wasn't worried, but didn't like the fact that he didn't know what was going on.

"Sara found a *Leptoceratops* skull five or six days ago," Laura said. "I tell you, that girl is just amazing at finding fossils. We're nearly done excavating it, but today Dave decided he wanted to help. Sara agreed on condition that he stop referring to himself and Sara as Bonnie and Clyde of the Back Country." She laughed. "They're so funny. Dave seems to bring out a carefree side of Sara."

Love in the Age of Dinosaurs

"I think there's some private joke going on, because Dave's been telling Sara all day what a *secret honour* it is to work with her and she keeps trying to shut him up." Sam chuckled. "Finally, just before we left, Dave asked if someone could pass him some water. Sara said, 'Let me do the *honours*,' and poured the full pitcher over his head. She said *secretly,* she'd been wanting to do that all day. Dave just laughed and said something about honour among thieves None of us get what that's about."

Thomas admitted to himself that he did not at all like the idea of Dave and Sara sharing private jokes or private anything else either.

"Here they come, now." Patrick pointed.

Dave and Sara were coming along the path. They were both dusty and bedraggled. Sara's pants were torn at the knee and Dave's shirt had a long black smear on it. They looked very tired, yet they were laughing and engaging in light-hearted banter.

"I do wish you'd stop calling it *Klepto*ceratops!" Sara laughed as she scolded.

"What's the matter? Haven't you ever had a dinosaur named after you before?" Dave grabbed Sara's swinging arm and waltzed her in a circle.

"Oh, hi, Tom. What hole did you crawl out of? I think this woman is trying to teach me a violent version of the Hokey Pokey. In Sara's choreography you stick your right hand in and... knock somebody's block off."

"I hear you two are thick as thieves these days." Tom took Sara's shovel from her hand and slipped her rucksack off her shoulder.

"You don't know the half of it, Tommy my boy." Dave winked at Sara. "Think of us as the pilferers of palaeontology, the scientific scions of shoplifting, the light-fingered looters of lost *Leptoceratops*."

"That is quite enough of that." Sara gave him a stern look.

"I'll put the gear away, if you two want to clean up and then get something to eat," Thomas offered.

"Oh, thanks." Sara said. As Thomas turned away he heard her say, "The light-fingered looters of lost *Leptoceratops*? I don't know what I'm going to do to you, but—"

"Now, now, Sara. There's no need for us to lock horns. Especially since *Kleptoceratops* doesn't have any. Let's just steal away peacefully to the dining tent and grab us some grub."

Sara's voice shook with laughter. "All right. Let's go eat. And for goodness sake, *be quiet.*"

"Like a thief in the night," said Dave solemnly.

As they entered the dining tent, Thomas saw Dave lean over and say something in Sara's ear. It must have been amusing, because she laughed as she replied. Dave laughed too and then the flap fell shut.

He quickly stowed the gear and headed back. He didn't know what precisely was going on between Dave and Sara, but he wanted to keep an eye on it.

As he ate, he answered questions about the symposium, but his mind was not really engaged. His thoughts were all centred on Sara. *She's beautiful. She has spent all day in the field, is tired, and dirty, and dressed in ragged, torn clothes, and yet I find her beautiful.*

He watched as she smiled, shrugged, gestured towards someone, became serious as she responded to someone else. *The many faces of Sara. So vibrant, so expressive.*

He remembered the outrage on her face the day they had met and he called her an underdressed teen-ager. It had changed

Love in the Age of Dinosaurs

to a cool aloofness when she tried to avoid answering his questions about her hitch-hiking. Over the last few weeks he'd seen enthusiasm and frustration, resentment and respect, wariness and uncertainty, joy and merriment. And then he thought of another expression that never failed to touch him. And he made his decision.

"Penny for them, Tom." Patrick had evidently been trying to get his attention for some time.

Thomas raised his brows.

"Look," Patrick said, softly enough that no one else could hear, "about this afternoon. Mary and I were way out of line. I know you don't want to get involved and I don't blame you. It's up to us to deal with the issue. And we will."

"You're saying I've managed at last to convince you it's not my affair, and the problem is yours alone to deal with as you see fit."

"That's right. You're off the hook, Tom."

"And there's where you're wrong," Thomas laughed mirthlessly, "I've been hooked all along. It just took me a while to realise it. Right now Sara needs a lot of support. But not just yours and Mary's.

"She also needs mine."

chapter

EIGHTEEN

Sara stretched out and listened to the breeze sough through the trees. It was still early, but it was going to be another hot day. The nylon tent was warm where the sun's rays brushed it. She stretched out a hand to touch its heat, in no hurry to move. Idle thoughts about what she needed to do today and what had been done the day before passed through her mind.

Dave was a lot of fun, as were the other team members, but she was also glad that Patrick and Thomas were back. The place just wasn't the same without them.

Especially Thomas.

That unwelcome realisation startled Sara and she immediately tamped it down. The previous night, she'd spent a good hour with Patrick after most of the others had gone to bed. He'd told her a bit about the conference he'd attended and a lot about Mary. She hadn't been put on bed-rest, but the doctor had told her to severely limit her physical activity. Patrick had admitted he worried about how she was frustrated by inactivity. "Thank goodness it's just four more weeks," he'd said. "I don't think Mary can stand much more."

I wish I could go and see her. We could just laze around all day together. I'm tired too. Reluctantly, she unzipped her sleeping bag and started hunting for her bathing suit.

I'm getting soft. I don't feel like getting up. I feel like I could sleep for a month. And I've no reason to be tired. Not like Mary.

She pulled on the leopard print suit and told herself to get a grip. She'd feel a lot more energetic after her swim. Grabbing her striped towel, she headed out to the stream. The water was quite cool, so, after calling a greeting to the others, she started swimming hard in an effort to warm up. The dip did its magic and after a nice hot shower, she felt refreshed and ready for a long, hard day's work.

"You look tired." Patrick waved her to join him at the table. "Are you feeling okay?"

"Yeah, I'm fine." She took a sip of milk. "You?"

"You did take a day off last week, didn't you? Thomas was pretty insistent, since you haven't taken any time off yet."

"Oh, well, as to that—" Hoping to distract him, she picked up her empty glass. "I think I'll go get more milk."

When she turned around, her way was blocked by another body. "Here, take this glass. I'll get another one." Thomas gave her a pleasant smile. "I can't wait to hear how you spent your free time. Be right back."

Love in the Age of Dinosaurs

Sara looked back. Patrick wasn't even trying to disguise his grin.

"On second thought, I really need to go use the washroom. I'll see you later."

Patrick caught her by the wrist. "Sit down and eat."

Sara was on the point of telling him to sod off when Thomas returned.

Thomas backed her into her chair. "Let's hear what you've been up to, Sara."

"Oh no," she said. "I shouldn't like to monopolise the conversation like that. Why don't you tell me all about the symposium? Who all was there?"

A slow grin spread across Thomas's face. "Andrew didn't make it after all, if that's what you're asking."

Sara felt her cheeks heat, but decided not to grace Thomas's statement with an answer. Neither he nor Patrick knew about Andrew's ultimatum and she planned to keep it that way. She was enormously relieved that Thomas and Andrew had not crossed paths.

"Don't look so relieved," Thomas said. "Andrew couldn't make it to the symposium, but he'll be at the funding meetings for sure. We'll have a lot to catch up on when we do meet."

Sara nearly choked on her toast. She hastily washed it down with the remainder of the milk. "Well, I'm done." She stood up and shrugged apologetically. "Early morning appointment with *Leptoceratops*, you know."

Thomas also stood. "Early morning appointment, yes. But not with *Leptoceratops*." He lightly grasped her hand. "With me. In the field office. In ten minutes. Be there."

Ten minutes later, Sara trudged over to the field office. She had no idea why Thomas wanted to see her. He couldn't possibly know about the funding application, could he? Surely he hadn't re-read the form before submitting it. Had he found out she didn't have Andrew's authorisation to work for him? Unlikely, because Andrew wasn't at the conference. What else could it be, then?

She stood in the doorway for a few seconds and watched Thomas work at the computer.

"Hi, Sara."

He hadn't looked up. Was he guessing?

"I saw you come up the path." He logged off and turned to face her. "I noticed you weren't exactly rushing. Not worried about being in trouble, were you?"

"Of course not. How could I be in trouble? I haven't done anything out of the ordinary."

"Nothing unusual?"

"Nothing." Too late, Sara realised the trap.

"So you didn't take any time off like I told you to."

She let her shoulders slump. "You know, that was not nice."

"Your ignoring my instructions or my calling you on it?"

Startled, Sara stared at Thomas for a moment as his mild words ricocheted around in her head. *Is that what he thinks of me? Is that how everyone sees me? Just some spoiled brat who never considers the feelings of others?*

Her stomach began to churn. She wasn't nice. Maybe she wasn't competent either. Was he going to sack her? "I'm sorry. I should have done as you asked."

"You're about to."

Sara swallowed and waited for the axe to fall.

Thomas laughed. "Don't look so nervous. You're not going into the field today. You need a break and I need some help in the office. Win-win for both of us."

Love in the Age of Dinosaurs

He pulled a USB drive out of the computer and handed it to her. "The articles on this drive are going into the Encyclopaedia of Dinosaurs. Could you proofread them and check the references? It needs to be done by noon."

Sara couldn't believe her ears. This was not dismissal. This was praise. Every palaeontologist on the planet wanted to contribute to Thomas's encyclopaedia. Being asked to help in any way was a privilege she had not expected. She beamed at Thomas. "Of course I can. With pleasure."

She opened the laptop on the corner desk and set to work immediately.

When she had finished, Thomas suggested they go canoeing on the Red Deer River. They walked down to the take-out in companionable silence. As they reached the canoes, Thomas said, "I'm checking out suitable sites for a documentary that's being filmed in the fall. He handed Sara a paddle. Part of the film will retrace the route Joseph Burr Tyrrell took in 1884 for the Geological Survey of Canada, when he was looking for coal deposits in the Red Deer River valley—"

"And found the first *Albertosaurus sarcophagus*," Sara said, as she fastened her life jacket.

"Precisely." Thomas smiled, pushing the canoe into the water and aiming it upstream. "And part of the filming will show other sites of interest throughout the park. So, I thought you and I could survey this area today. Hopefully we'll do it without all the flies and mosquitoes that plagued Tyrrell and his expedition."

Thomas examined the sky. "It's supposed to rain later, but we'll be back before then. You take the bow seat."

Sara settled herself smoothly and quickly onto the bow seat. The centre of the canoe was filled with two rolled-up painters, a bailer, a tow rope, and a spare paddle. The ditty bag Thomas had filled with a tarp, a first aid kit, some food and water, a small blanket, a camera and a pair of binoculars was also there.

They paddled upstream for a while in companionable silence, the only sounds the dipping of the paddles and the oo-wah-hoo-oo-oo of Mourning Doves and the tweetings of Rock Wrens. A couple of Prairie Falcons swooped overhead. As they travelled past striped rock formations, Sara spotted a Golden Eagle soaring against the deep blue of a vast sky only lightly streaked with wispy cirrus clouds.

Far in the distance, cumulus clouds were merging to form big wads like cotton batting. Sara turned to beam at Thomas. "I love this, and I haven't done it in a very long time. We used to…Oh, Thomas, look at the Cliff Swallows! I love the way they fly, they're such little acrobats, flitting and dipping and darting!"

A couple of times, they beached the canoe and went walking through the cottonwoods growing by the river. Once they inadvertently got too close to a nest of goslings, and beat a hasty retreat when the goose protested. Late in the afternoon they pulled onto a sandy beach, where they shared grapes and water and trail mix. Thomas spread the blanket and they lay side-by-side watching the clouds overhead.

Sara was dreamily following some fluffy white clouds scudding quickly across the sky. As one of them changed from a turtle into kitten she felt a sudden chill breeze. She looked towards the north and saw darker clouds. She said lazily, "On the way to the lake, we used to—" She stopped and covered her eyes.

"Used to what?" Thomas retracted the hand that had been hovering over Sara's shapely leg. Her mood seemed to have shifted. The laughter in her eyes had fled, supplanted by a wistful expression that lingered just long enough to tug at his heart-

Love in the Age of Dinosaurs

strings before it too vanished and was replaced by a bleak stoicism. Without having moved an inch, Sara seemed suddenly more distant.

"Oh, nothing." Her laughter sounded forced. "I'm just babbling, not even thinking about what I'm saying."

Thomas rolled onto his side and looked directly at her. "That's okay. I like babbling. As you were saying…"

"I can't remember any more." Sara raised herself onto one elbow and looked out over the water. "Is that a beaver?"

Sure enough, a big beaver was swimming by, pulling a large leafy branch. He watched it swim out of sight before he turned back to Sara and gently brushed his fingers up her arm. "Why don't you tell me what you used to do? Twice this afternoon you've started to tell me something, and then you've changed the subject."

Sara looked everywhere but at his face. She bit her lower lip, but didn't say anything.

He gently grasped her chin and forced her to face him. "Why don't you tell me what you used to do?"

Sara shrugged. "There's nothing to tell. I've no intention of boring you to death with silly little reminiscences."

"They're not silly little reminiscences and I wouldn't be bored to death." He softened his tone and said persuasively, "C'mon, Sara, I want to hear them."

"Another time perhaps." She looked up at the sky. "Maybe we should get going. Some of those clouds look quite dark." Far in the distance there was a flash of light followed by a low rumble. "There's a storm coming. We need to get going."

She began to gather things up. She had a faraway, closed expression on her face that telegraphed her desire to withdraw into herself, far away from him. Thomas understood it and he came close to abiding it. About to stand, he suddenly changed his mind. Instead, he stayed on the blanket. "We'll go as soon as you've told me what you were going to say."

Sara shook her head in disbelief and pointed at the sky. "You're joking. If we don't get moving, we're going to be caught in that storm. And I don't want to be caught in that storm. I want to go. Now."

Thomas gave an indifferent shrug. "Want all you like. We're not leaving until you tell me what I want to know." He winced inwardly as she shot him a look as warm and pleasant as a poisoned arrow through the heart.

"Stay then." She headed for the canoe.

Thomas was on his feet in a flash. He caught her upper arm. "Oh, I don't think so, Sara." He took a quick look at the darkening skies before retrieving the blanket and the other items they'd brought ashore. With them held with one arm and his other hand still holding on to Sara, he marched her to where an overhanging rocky ledge offered some protection from the approaching storm.

"Let me go!" Sara tried unsuccessfully to remove her arm from his grasp.

"I said 'No'," Thomas told her calmly. "At the risk of my sounding repetitive, we are not going anywhere until you've told me what I want to know."

He pulled her down beside him on the sand. Unable to break his hold and move away, Sara lifted her chin, clamped her lips tightly together and glared at him wrathfully.

He studied her for a minute or two, waiting for her shoulders to slump in defeat. When they finally did, he released her and said pleasantly, "So what is it that you used to do?"

"Many things, none of which are any of your business."

Love in the Age of Dinosaurs

Thomas sighed and said gently, "Tell me what you used to do, Sara. We're not leaving until I'm satisfied."

Sara sat for a long time without answering. Finally, she said, "Fine. Have it your way. I'm sure this scintillating tidbit of information will just knock your socks off it's so exciting.

"My brother and I used to go canoeing together. And we always spent the time pointing out to each other the different shapes that we saw in the clouds.

"Satisfied? Let's go!"

"No."

"I've told you what you wanted to know. Now I want to go."

"You've only told me one of the things I want to know. I want to know lots of other things, too."

Sara's throat tightened. Keeping her gaze locked on his face, she closed her fingers on a fistful of sand and tensed in readiness for springing up.

As if he'd read her thoughts, Thomas closed his hand around her wrist and gave one firm shake.

Sara's fingers opened involuntarily and the sand sifted harmlessly back down to the earth.

Thomas watched her without expression.

Her legs began to shake. "Can't we do this some other time? I really, really don't want to do this right now. Please, Thomas, let's just go."

"No," he said again.

Sara wrapped her arms around her shins and rested her head on her bent knees. Her chest was so tight she had trouble breathing. Thoughts went spinning through her head, until she felt dizzy and nauseous. She forced herself to take several deep breaths.

He watched her impassively. Would he recognize a panic attack if he saw one? God, she hoped not. She had to get herself under control.

Sara did. After several minutes, she lifted her head from her knees and looked at Thomas.

He handed her the water bottle. "Have a drink. It might help."

"I don't want to do this, Thomas." She was so very, very tired. "It's not going to change anything. Please let's just go now."

Thomas gently brushed hair away from her face. "I know you don't want to, and I'm sorry. But this is the way it has to be."

She drew back and glared at him with loathing. "I hate you."

"That's okay. Better to hate me than to hate life or to hate yourself."

She flinched, because what he said hurt more than anything had for a long time.

"That's it, isn't it, Sara? You hate yourself. Is it because you survived and they all died?"

"You haven't a clue what you're talking about. So why don't you...Leave. Me. Alone."

"Leave you alone? To do what? Work yourself to death?" His voice was as hot with anger as hers had been cold with desolation. "Because that's what you're doing, isn't it? You neglect your health, focus exclusively on work to the detriment of everything else, and drive yourself far past the point of exhaustion, and to what end? Not a happy one, that's for sure."

"I don't seek a happy end, don't worry about that. I'm not such a fool as to think that I deserve to be happy."

Love in the Age of Dinosaurs

Thomas put his hands on her shoulders and shook her. "Why don't you seek happiness? You deserve it as much as anyone else."

"Right."

Fat drops of rain began to pelt the sand. Thomas pulled her closer, so she was under the overhanging rock, and close enough to feel his body warmth. "What do you mean, 'right'? Your family died, and they died terribly, Sara. I'm sorry for it, and if there were anything I could do to change it, I would. But it's not within my power.

"For whatever reasons, their time here was done, and for whatever reason, yours is not, and that is why you find yourself still among the living. Why don't you deserve the happiness that life has in store for you?"

Hysterical laughter fought to escape Sara's throat. "For whatever reasons? I'll tell you the reason. They died because I killed them. And one doesn't go about killing one's family and then expecting to live happily ever after."

Thomas gripped Sara's shoulders hard. "What are you talking about? A drunk driver killed your family. You weren't even there."

The threatening laughter turned to sobs and burst forth. "That's why they died. Because *I wasn't there*." The tears she'd held back now began to stream down her face. She put every ounce of self-loathing she felt into her voice. "I was busy working in the lab. Not on anything essential, really. As usual, I was so wrapped up in my work, that I couldn't bring myself to leave when I was supposed to. So instead of going with Mum and Alex to meet my dad at the airport, I called and said I'd meet them all at home. That is why I wasn't in the car, Thomas. I wasn't driving when they were probably too tired to avoid a drunk driver."

"It wasn't some grand design of some greater power. It wasn't some fluke accident of fate."

She laughed bitterly. "The fates don't make mistakes. They weave a warp faced design with coarse and roughened threads. But if the fates are not kind, at least they are appropriate. I made my choice that day. What do I need a family for? I have my work. And in one of the great ironies of life, that is what is left to me. My work.

"And so I work, Thomas. I work and work and work." She covered her face and let herself weep.

When her sobs quieted, he handed her some tissues. "We can't change our destinies, Sara. None of us has the power to alter fate. When we've finished whatever it is that we are destined to do or learn here, we're done. And we move on to whatever comes next. It was time for your family to move on. Whether you were there or not made no difference. Their time had come. Yours had not. So fate's design was interlaced with finer yarn to create a balanced weave after all."

Sara attempted a smile. "I wish I could believe that."

"You must," Thomas said. "Otherwise there is no point to anything. You were granted life to fulfill some purpose. It's only through living that you will discover what it is you're meant to do. It's the same for all of us."

"Sara," Thomas said after they'd sat quietly for several minutes, "who used to sing 'Follow Me'? Why does the song make you so sad?"

Sara looked down at her hands and then up again. "My mother. When I was little, before Alex was born, we'd go out together for walks or to the playground or shopping. She insisted I hold her hand so I wouldn't get lost. And she'd sing the words of the chorus."

Love in the Age of Dinosaurs

"When Alex was small, I did the same thing with him. Later, sometimes she'd be trying to hustle us out the door for school or whatever and we'd sing it back to her." She shook her head and blinked back tears. "Such a silly sad memory. My mind is full of them. All the things that used to make us the happiest are the things I can't bear to think about now."

"And the campfires," Thomas said. "Tell me about the campfires."

Sara could barely see the river through the sheet of rain that was now falling. She kept staring straight ahead and tried to speak past the lump in her throat. "We always had campfires when I was a kid. Wiener roasts at school picnics; bonfires at campgrounds when we went tenting. We had an outdoor fireplace at the lake. Alex and I liked roasting hot dogs on sticks. We both liked to get them really black and crunchy on the outside.

"After we'd eaten, we'd put the sticks back in the fire and try to light them. It didn't always work, because the sticks were always pretty green. There'd be lots of popping and crackling and sparks exploding everywhere and we'd point the glowing ends of our sticks up at the sky and write our names among the stars." Her voice caught, and she paused to swallow. "Later, when we were a bit older and could recognise the constellations, we drew our own personal constellations up there beside Cassiopeia and Draco and Cepheus."

"What designs did you draw?" There was a smile in Thomas's voice.

The sobs she hadn't been able to hold back had made her hoarse. "My designs were always elaborate. Dolphins, and unicorns, and dinosaurs, and lionesses. Eventually, after we went to Egypt, I settled on an ankh." She fell silent for a moment, remembering. "But not Alex. All he ever wanted was a simple circle." She swallowed again, feeling the soreness in her throat. "When I asked him why, he said, 'Because of what it represents'."

Her eyes filled with tears again, and she couldn't blink them away. "I thought I understood, so I didn't ask him what he meant."

She swiped at the tears sliding down her cheeks. "And now I never can."

She released the tight hold she'd kept on herself for so long and began to cry in earnest. She wept in sorrow and anger and guilt and a loneliness so deep that she doubted her soul would ever break the surface and breathe again. She wept with great wracking sobs for all that made the world forlorn. For what is not taken and for what is not given.

The sobs deepened, changed, became a high-pitched eerie keening, a primal lament that sent echoes of despair and anguish and emptiness out to maim the night. Sara wailed her loss, her loneliness, her emptiness to the sky where once she had traced the stars.

When the last plaints of her despair were swallowed by the dark, the only sound left to disturb the deep stillness of the night was a robin perched atop a cottonwood singing his promises to his love. He sang as though his heart were bursting. All night long he sang his song while Sara slept.

chapter

NINETEEN

Sara moved and slowly opened her eyes. Her head was resting on Thomas's chest.

Her eyes felt prickly and swollen and she had a headache, but she felt lighter somehow, as if a stone somewhere deep inside had shifted. She eased away from Thomas and finally looked up to meet his steady gaze.

Her voice shook when she said, "Well I guess that's one way of drowning my sorrows. I'm so sorry, Thomas. I don't know what came over me."

"Grief. Pure and simple grief. It had to express itself sometime, Sara. You couldn't go on holding it inside forever. It was destroying you." He hugged her tightly. "And that I couldn't bear."

He released her and said, "We'd better go. They'll all be wondering what has happened to us."

They walked in silence back to the canoe.

At the take-out, they were met by several members of the team. "We were just heading out to look for you," said Dave.

Patrick took one look at her and silently held out his hand. She grasped it and he pulled her into his chest and hugged her closely. His arm around her shoulders, he led her back toward his tent.

Behind her, she heard Dave say, "You look like you could use a hot breakfast, Tom."

By the time Sara returned to her own tent a couple of hours later, the camp had emptied. She walked over to the dining tent to talk to Dave. He told her that Thomas wanted to spend the afternoon prospecting with her and Patrick. Until then, she was free.

Sara filled the time by taking a very hot shower and then eating the very hot breakfast that Dave insisted on cooking for her. After that, since the thermometer had reached thirty degrees and was still rising, she decided to do some laundry. She finished hanging out the clothes on the line that she and Laura and Sam had strung between some cottonwoods and picked up the bucket of rinse water to toss into the bush. At that moment, Barney came bouncing out in front of her, and in an effort to miss the dog, she turned and tossed the water the other way, soaking Thomas from his chest to his knees.

Sara had to laugh. Thomas's tee-shirt and cargo shorts were completely plastered to his body. A very lean and muscular body. He hadn't shaved, and the shadow of his beard, plus his crooked grin gave him a slightly piratical air.

"Oh, sorry, Tom," she said. "I didn't want to hit the dog."

Love in the Age of Dinosaurs

Thomas kept walking towards her, a wide wicked smile on his face. "Really? You didn't want to get the dog wet? So you decided to drown your boss?"

Sara backed up. There was still an inch or two of water in the pail. "I guess we shouldn't let this go to waste." She tossed the rest at Thomas, but completely missed him.

He lunged. "You're in hot water now."

Sara dropped the bucket and ran.

She'd taken only a few steps when Thomas hooked his fingers into the waist band of her shorts and pulled her up short.

"Hmm," he said, "I think we're going to have to streamline your plans for the morning." He started dragging her down the path.

"No fair." Sara tried unsuccessfully to squirm her way free. "I didn't even get you. I totally missed. It was an accident."

"Missing me? An accident? Finally! A claim that holds water. Just like you're about to!" He tossed her into the stream, and kicking off his shoes, jumped in beside her. When he surfaced, Sara splashed water in his face and started swimming away. Four strokes later, Thomas's hand closed around her ankle and he tugged her back against his chest. "Not so fast. We have some unfinished business to attend to." He propelled her to the sandy bank, where he straddled her and pinned her down.

"Hey! You're getting sand in my hair."

"Don't worry about it. I'll give you a good dunking later and that'll wash it out."

Sara looked into his cornflower eyes. "A dunking? You could try being nice, you know. I wouldn't protest."

Thomas's smile broadened. "No protest? Well, in that case, I shall try to be nice." He pressed his lips onto hers. When he pulled back a few moments later, he repeated softly, "Very nice is what I'll be."

As his lips descended once more onto hers, Sara closed her eyes and showed Thomas just how nice she could be when the occasion called for it. After a while, she thought she heard voices. "You know, we shouldn't—"

"Yes, we should," Thomas deepened his kiss. "I've been wanting to do this since the day we met."

Sara gave herself up completely to the moment. *It's nice being nice.*

As Thomas caressed her, Sara sank deeper into a dreamy lethargy. She lost awareness of anything but him. She became numb to the water lapping over her legs, only feeling the warmth where his skin touched hers. He stroked her hip, sending chills up her spine. She responded by trailing her fingers gently over his hardened muscles. He groaned slightly and crushed her to him. He deepened his kiss.

The feel of his lips on hers felt better than anything she'd ever felt before and she could not get enough. A primal urge to surrender her entire being surged out of nowhere. She completely lost track of who she was, who she had been. She and Thomas were alone in a world of their own making. She wasn't even aware that she was on the bank of the stream until a sharp whistle cut through the air and penetrated her consciousness. Immediately, she felt grains of sand embedded in her back and water on her legs.

She opened her eyes and saw Dave and Patrick looking down on them from the path. Mortified, she pushed Thomas off her and started swimming so fast towards the camp that he didn't catch her up until the last bend in the stream.

Love in the Age of Dinosaurs

"It can't have been anything I said," he said as they climbed out of the water.

Sara felt the blood surge to her face. "Sorry. Dave and Patrick were on the path and they saw us."

"And they left? Wow! My performance must really need work if I cleared the theatre that quickly." His grin was rueful. "It wouldn't be so bad if it were just the viewers, but to have the co-star bail, too, well, it can only mean I'm sadly out of practice." He pulled Sara close and kissed her gently. "I'll have to rectify that. Evening rehearsal after supper, Sara. Be prepared for it to run late." He turned on his heel and headed toward his tent.

Sara entered her own tent and peeled off her wet things. She smiled as she thought of Thomas's parting words, but burned with embarrassment when she remembered what Dave and Patrick must have seen.

She herself was shocked at her behaviour this morning. *I don't want to lead Thomas on and I definitely do not want to get romantically involved with him. So why did I let him kiss me?*

The answer that surged from the depths of her being left her shaken and unhappy. *You're in love with him. All he has to do is smile at you in that intimate way and you're putty in his hands. And didn't it feel good?!*

As Sara dressed, she adjured herself to get a grip. *You are not to fall for this guy. If you got him, you would lose him. You lose everyone. Some people are just meant to be alone. So suck it up and get over him.* She put on shoes and socks, so she'd be ready to go prospecting right after lunch. She'd grab her hat later. As she hung her wet clothes on the line, they flapped in the breeze. Gambolling like naughty children, they taunted, *Too Late. You're Hooked. Ha-Ha.*

For Sara, it seemed like a prelude to the teasing that was undoubtedly in store for her at lunch. If it weren't for the fact that she'd only be delaying the inevitable, she'd skip all her meals for the rest of the summer. She groaned inwardly and decided just to get it over with.

Sara and Thomas filled their plates and were taking their seats in the dining tent, when Dave remarked, "Well, you're both looking refreshed and positively radiant with—Ow!" He rubbed his ear and shot an indignant look at Patrick. "That hurt."

The next moment he grinned unrepentantly and turned once more to Thomas and Sara.

"Dave," said Patrick warningly.

"Ah, geez. Just when I thought Tom was well and truly slain by love, he resurrects himself in Pat's body with Pat's voice and the flat of Pat's hand."

"Oh, don't let Patrick stop you, Dave. Go ahead and tell me what's on your mind. I'm sure that you'll enjoy my response as much as Pat's. In fact, I'm planning something very special for you."

"Oh, back to planning, are we?" Dave stepped out of arm's reach. "What happened to spontaneity? Judging by the preview this morning—"

"The next performance, while expected to be spectacular, is unfortunately going to be privately aired. Sorry to disappoint you, Dave, but there just aren't any tickets available."

"I don't think I'm the one you should worry about disappointing," Dave retorted. "I'd be more worried about—Hey, where'd Sara go?"

"She said to tell you both that neither the preview nor the reviews made her want to pay the admission to the performance," Patrick said. "Apparently, her schedule is full for the rest of the summer, although she can spare the time to go prospecting this afternoon. I think the way she put it was, 'I'm definitely holding out for better prospects.'"

"Well, no one can say you've lost your touch, Tom." Dave bent double with laughter. "Or come to think of it, maybe you have."

He tried to beat a hasty retreat behind Patrick, who merely said, 'I warned you,' before stepping aside to allow Thomas free access.

Much later, she overheard Dave say that of the many painful experiences he had endured over the summer, that particular moment was by far the worst.

Undecided whether to be amused or indignant, Sara returned to her tent to collect what she needed for prospecting. She was waiting when Thomas and Patrick turned up at the field office.

"Ready?" Thomas asked.

Sara nodded and held up her awl and a whisk broom before stowing them in her rucksack. Patrick had the handheld GPS and Thomas threw a couple of light pick axes into the back of the Jeep.

"Everyone got water?" asked Thomas.

Sara showed him her full bottle.

With Thomas at the wheel, they headed for the southeast quadrant. After thirty minutes of driving, he parked and they trekked into a steep-sided ravine. They hiked in the erosion channels, keeping their eyes peeled for broken bone fragments that would have been washed downwards with precipitation and run-off.

Patrick found some bone particles, but when they traced them uphill to the source, all they found was a bone too fragmented to ever be glued together again. "Well, this won't tell us much." Patrick sounded disappointed. "We'd better go back down."

On the way back, Sara discovered the dome-shaped skull cap of a *Stegoceras*, but further digging around it produced no other bones. She recorded its position with the GPS and they worked together to dig it out.

They continued to explore the ravine, but only Thomas found anything worthwhile, some large teeth of a carnivore.

"Well, that wraps it up for today." Thomas indicated the shadows on the ravine walls. "We'd better get back."

Back at camp, they unloaded the equipment and stored it in the field office shed. Together they walked companionably to the dining tent, where most of the others had already filled their plates.

"What a day," Laura groaned when Sara sat beside her. "We prospected for hours and hours and found nothing. My back is killing me."

Sara stretched wearily. "Yeah. Same with us. I'm dead on my feet."

"You look as if you didn't get much sleep last night." Sam looked closely at Sara. "Everything okay?"

Sara smiled, touched by her concern. "Yeah. Thanks for asking. Everything's fine. I'm just tired, that's all."

"So what happened yesterday?" Laura said. "Thomas usually has his storm radar pretty finely tuned."

"Yeah," agreed Sam. "He never gets caught out in a storm unless he wants to."

"Neither of us wanted to," Sara admitted ruefully. "We just didn't have a choice. The rain started suddenly and we had to take shelter and wait it out." She yawned. "It was a rough night."

She stood, hoping to end the questioning. At least they don't know anything about this morning. I guess Dave was discreet after all. "I'm going to bed. See you tomorrow."

chapter

TWENTY

Over the next few days, the team was divided into groups of two or three to go prospecting in various sections of the park. Sara was teamed with Mike and Geoff at first, but on the fifth morning, she began a rotation with Sam and Laura.

Thomas caught them before they set out. He indicated an area on the map. "I want you to stay in this section, because you're going to a fairly remote area of the park and I want to know where you are."

As he walked them to the Jeep, he added, "A severe weather system is supposed to move in by mid-afternoon. You should be back here by three." He pulled Sara aside, and said, "I mean it. As soon as it starts to rain, come back here immediately. Clear?"

"Yeah, okay. If it starts to rain, we'll come right back."

Once in their designated area, they concentrated their efforts on a coulee that looked promising, but failed to yield anything worthwhile. Sara suggested they head farther south, toward the park boundary. It was well past noon and storm clouds were building up in the north.

"I guess we have time." Sam frowned at the sky. "The storm doesn't seem to be too close yet?" Then she shrugged. "Well, we won't be long. If we get a bit wet, we get a bit wet."

"That's the spirit! I just have a feeling that that's the area we need to focus on," Sara said.

Laura said, "You have a feeling about it? What are we waiting for then?"

They walked for an hour or so until they reached a promising ravine. They spread out. Sara went to the right. Within minutes, she found something interesting. She bent to look closer and began picking at the soil.

She began to hum. She definitely had a large and possibly very unusual fossil here. She called to Laura and Sam. They hurried over and began to help chisel away rock—a not too difficult task as the volcanic ash broke off in nice chunks.

A couple of hours passed as they continued digging. Sara noticed that the wind had picked up, but wasn't going to stop. If they left the fossil half-uncovered and heavy rain fell, they might never find it again. She continued to dig, working as fast as she could and still take care.

"What do you think it is?" Sam said, when enough of the shell was visible that they knew it was some sort of a turtle.

"Well, I'm pretty sure it's not a giant tortoise. What do you think?" Sara paused to stretch.

Love in the Age of Dinosaurs

"My guess is *Basilemys*," Laura replied. "Could you hand me the GPS? Thanks. I think we'd better get a location and cover it for now."

As they finished covering the turtle, a light rain began to fall. By the time they reached the Jeep, it was raining heavily. They threw their gear in the back and hopped in just as a zigzag of lightning lit up the sky. It was followed almost immediately by a loud clap of thunder, and the smell of ozone filled the air. Immediately the clouds split open and released a deluge that reduced visibility to zero.

"We're not going anywhere until this eases off." Sam had started the engine, but now she turned it off.

They sat in silence, unable to play the radio or to hear each other talk while lightning cracked and thunder boomed all around them. Two hours elapsed before the storm abated slightly. Thunder still rumbled and the rain continued to fall heavily, but the lightning was no longer directly overhead.

Laura, who had been dozing in the back seat, leaned forward and said, "Maybe we'd better start thinking about getting back. Anyone know what time it is?"

"Six by my watch," Sam said.

"Are you sure? Let me see it." Sara grasped Sam's wrist and peered at the watch.

Sam started the engine and began carefully negotiating what remained of the road. "Maybe we'd better start brainstorming about what we're going to tell Thomas. It's just possible that he isn't going to be too happy about how late we are."

"By the way," Laura said, "I've been meaning to ask. What did he say to you just before we left?"

"He said that we were to come back at the first sign of rain." Sara chewed pensively on her lower lip. "And that's what we tried to do, right? As soon as it started to rain, we started back."

"Well, strictly speaking, it is the truth," Sam said at last.

"Yeah. It is the truth. Strictly speaking." When no one said anything, Laura added, "I think that's what we should say if we're asked."

"So when do you think we should tell him about the turtle?" Sam said. "The *what* might make him happy, but I'm not too sure about the *where*. What do you think, Sara?"

Sara groaned. "Actually, I really *really* do not want to think about that at all."

"Well, I don't know why we're worrying so much about it. Thomas is one of the most reasonable people I know." She patted Sara's shoulder. "He couldn't possibly think that it's your fault we were stuck out here in this storm, could he?"

Sara smiled weakly. She thought it quite likely that he could.

It was nearly dark when they drove into camp. By the time they wearily climbed out, the Jeep was surrounded by the entire team. No one said a word, not even to ask why they were so late. Rob and Alan silently gathered up the equipment and headed off to the shed with it.

Thomas stepped forward and said, "I'd like to see the three of you in the office. Now."

"Sure, Tom," said Sam. "Sorry, everyone, if we've worried you. We did start back when it began to rain, but we still got caught in it."

Laura and Sara added their apologies.

As they followed Thomas, Sara's mood vacillated between pessimistic and more pessimistic. Optimism about the coming interview completely eluded her.

Love in the Age of Dinosaurs

How's a person supposed to think positive when he looks more menacing than the thunderclouds that dumped all over us? He really could work a little harder at appearing approachable.

She was strongly tempted to tell Thomas that she had just remembered a prior engagement. After stealing a glance at his face, though, she decided it wasn't quite the moment to toss his way a lofty *I'll see you shortly. I just have to go and powder my nose.* She also briefly considered and rejected a simple *Aw, if you're so interested in how people get drenched, go jump in the lake, Thomas.*

She had just settled on running as the best possible option when his fingers clamped onto the back of her neck in what not even the most positive of thinkers would describe as a caress.

When they reached the office, Thomas sat behind his desk and waited for them to seat themselves in front of it. Then he asked for an explanation so formally that Sara knew her worst fears were about to be realised.

The women looked at one another. Sara cleared her throat. "Well..."

Thomas raised an eyebrow. "Thank you, Sara. I think I'd like to hear Sam and Laura's version of the tale first, if you don't mind."

She closed her mouth, not sure whether to be relieved or worried.

Her uncertainty evaporated when he said, "There will be plenty of time later for your explanation, Sara. You can be sure I will give you my strictest attention. For as long as it takes."

Sara attempted a weak smile. "Uh, thanks."

Thomas listened to Sam and Laura without interrupting. He seemed pleased about the *Basilemys* and he nodded once or twice as they described the storm and their decision to wait it out. Sara was just starting to believe that he was satisfied with their explanation when he began to ask a few unnecessary and pointed questions about where they had actually gone and what time they had gone there and why.

Sam and Laura did their best, but as Thomas summed everything up, the last wispy fringes of Sara's optimism floated gloomily away.

"So what you're telling me is that you ignored the meteorology report and my instructions. It was time for you to return to camp. Storm clouds moved in. You left your assigned area, but instead of returning here, as you were instructed to do, you moved into an unassigned area. All this because Sara had a hunch that there were better pickings to be had in an area that you all knew was off-limits. Once there, you risked your lives for the sake of a fossil that was well enough covered to be excavated at a later date when the weather improved."

Sara winced. *Should have seen that one coming.* It wasn't the first time Thomas had demonstrated how unappreciative he was of the extreme effort it took to try and obscure the obvious. And, as usual, he was totally unconcerned about the effect his astuteness had on others. *Imagine how much happier a place the world would be if Thomas had only taken up smoking instead of this nasty little habit of going directly to the heart of the matter. He sure has no appreciation for any embellishment of the plain facts. He always has to have the sharp, unadorned edges of the unvarnished truth. And then when he gets it, does he keep it to himself? No, even though you express no desire for it, he throws the stark, unvarnished truth right back at you.*

Sam and Laura exchanged a look. "Well, when you put it like that," began Sam, "I guess..."

"Well, it wasn't quite..." Laura, too, failed to complete the thought.

Love in the Age of Dinosaurs

"Right! I don't have to tell you I'm not pleased. So for the remainder of the week, you have new assignments. Laura, you're working with Alan. Sam, you're with Geoff."

He came around the desk and smiled suddenly. "But I am glad you're safely back. And good work with the *Basilemys*. You're probably starving, so you'd better go and get something to eat."

Looking relieved, Laura and Sam got up to go. Sara quickly stood as well.

"Not so fast, Sara. I'm not through with you yet."

Sara sat on the edge of her chair and watched him warily.

Thomas leaned against the desk, arms crossed, and regarded Sara for a full minute. "So what have you got to say for yourself?"

Sara sat back in the chair. She was not fond of questions like that. They sounded innocuous enough, but hidden perils often surfaced in the most unpleasant ways. She selected and rejected several responses before finally settling on silence as the safest answer.

"Maybe you'd like to say a word or two about these hunches of yours that provide you with such interesting experiences," Thomas suggested.

"Uh, no, I don't really think so. I have a strong hunch that that would not make for riveting conversation."

Thomas raised his eyebrow. Then his face relaxed and his beautiful smile appeared. "Good point. Maybe we've done enough talking for the moment. There are other things to focus on right now besides conversation. Come here." He held out his arms.

Sara stepped into them. He tilted her head back and kissed her hard.

"I'm glad you're back," he murmured huskily. He raised his head for a second and then kissed her again, this time more gently, but no less enthusiastically.

Sara's last coherent thought was that Thomas was nothing if not full of surprises.

Fifteen minutes later, she had completely abandoned reason and surrendered to instinct.

Thomas suddenly removed his lips from Sara's breast and yanked her shirt back down. He zipped up her jeans. He stood quickly and pulled Sara to her feet.

"That's enough of that." He sounded disgustingly cheerful. "We mustn't get too carried away. I still have to tell you about your assignment for the rest of the week."

Surprised by his sudden change, Sara dazedly reined in her own desires. She straightened her dishevelled clothing and, with a supreme effort, turned her thoughts away from pleasure and back to work. "Will I be working with you?"

"No, not with me. With Dave."

"With Dave?" Her first thought was that she had misheard. "Okay. Where do you want me to take him? I assume we'll be focussing on basic techniques and I'll show—"

"I think you have misunderstood. I did not say that Dave would be working with you. I said that *you* would be working with *Dave*. I expect that will mean hauling a lot of water, chopping a lot of wood, peeling a lot of potatoes and scrubbing a lot of pots."

Sara stared at Thomas for a full minute without saying a single word.

"You...you..." She struggled to find her voice. "You are assigning me to the kitchen?"

"Yeah. I believe that's what I said."

"You. Cannot. Be. Serious."

"Can't I? Why not?" Thomas appeared genuinely interested in her answer.

"You know very well why not! I'm a trained palaeontologist. I am not supposed to be a scullery maid. I'm supposed to be helping you. I'm supposed to be digging up fossils and lending a hand with prospecting."

"Yes, that is exactly the point," Thomas agreed. "You are supposed to be helping me, not traipsing off on your own, endangering yourself and others because you have some half-baked ideas about where the next fossil is coming from."

"Half-baked ideas!" Sara bristled. "My hunches are not half-baked ideas!"

"Well, perhaps I was wrong to call them half-baked."

"Thank you," Sara replied icily, although she was somewhat mollified.

"Because that is far too complimentary a description of them," Thomas continued. "Yes, it's true that you located an amazing sinkhole. But only by sliding into it and giving yourself a severe abrasion in the process. You're just lucky that that was your only injury.

"We don't need to go into what could have happened if we hadn't been lucky enough to find you. And then there was the *Troodon,* uncovered at the risk of severe dehydration.

"And today, the *Basilemys* unearthed in an unsheltered area in the middle of an electrical storm. A positively electrifying discovery, that one."

"We got back to the car before the lightning," Sara muttered. "We weren't really in much danger."

"You won't be in *any* danger in the kitchen. So get ready to embark on your new career—gourmet cooking on an open fire—because that's where you're assigned until I say otherwise."

"Are you firing me?"

"Not a chance."

"Then I quit!" Sara headed for the door.

"I wouldn't advise it." His tone was entirely reasonable. "You really don't want to get a reputation for breaking your contracts. You do recall that you signed a contract with me?"

Sara stopped in her tracks. She couldn't believe her ears. The insufferable man had her over the proverbial barrel. If she broke her contract, she might never get another job.

She took several deep breaths and tried a new tack. "Okay, Thomas," she said, calmly as she could. She turned around and retraced her steps. "I understand you're angry and I agree you have good reason to be."

"I'm not angry."

"Then what are you?"

"Terrified. Terrified of what you'll get up to alone or with others while I'm gone to the funding meetings."

"You're joking."

"Actually, I'm not."

Sara sat back down in her chair. Finally she said, "Look, Thomas. It's been a bad day. Could we just put it behind us and go back to the way things were before?"

Thomas smiled. "Sure. Absolutely. We were both enjoying ourselves. We can definitely go back to that. I'm looking forward to it."

"Good!" Sara stood up. "So where am I working tomorrow?"

"In the kitchen with Dave."

She wanted to kick him. "But, Thomas, I'm good in the field."

"I do know that, Sara. You are one of the best hands I have ever had in the field."

"Well, then—"

"But for the next few days you'll be working hand in hand with Dave."

Sara slumped into the chair. "Fine." She still wanted an explanation. "Then why did you and I—well, you know—why did you decide to do that just before you demoted me?"

"Well, I could hardly do it after," Thomas said reasonably. "I didn't think you'd be in the mood when you found out where you're going." He paused and graced her with his sweetest smile. "I do think it was one of my better *hunches*, don't you?"

"You are a despicable ogre."

Thomas looked at his watch. "And you, Cinderella, are late for work. I know for a fact that there is a mound of dishes awaiting your loving ministrations. You'd better be on your way if you want to be back in your tent before midnight."

Sara stomped to the dining tent, muttering many uncomplimentary things about Thomas McBride.

chapter

TWENTY-ONE

The next morning Dave welcomed Sara to the kitchen so warmly that she released her resentment and began to enjoy herself. He put her in charge of making the oatmeal porridge, while he handled everything else with admirable proficiency. Barney put in an appearance and seemed positively overjoyed that Sara was now involved in food preparation.

"We're going to need double the supplies if you keep on feeding him like that." Dave tossed a piece of cooked bacon over to the dog. "But hey, we can't let Thomas's poor starving pet go hungry, can we?"

Thomas came in and helped himself to a large bowl of porridge. After a few bites he said, "Hey, what's with all the lumps? Didn't Dave give you any instructions?"

Sara had privately been a little disappointed at how the porridge had turned out. She looked thoughtfully over at Dave.

He met her gaze with a clear-eyed one of his own and winked, firmly cementing for all time his place in her affections.

"Actually, Thomas," she said with perfect honestly, "I thought I was following Dave's directions to the letter. I'm a bit of a novice at cooking, but I want you to know that I am completely committed to learning everything that Dave has to offer." She paused and then added sweetly, "And I look forward to sharing all of my new-found knowledge with you."

"I'll bet you do," Thomas acknowledged with a laugh.

As Sara walked away, she heard him say to Patrick. "Good thing I like lumpy porridge."

After breakfast, the team dispersed to their various tasks. On his way out, Thomas stopped to talk to Dave and Sara, who had begun the washing up. "It's supposed to rain again, in which case we might all end up back here sooner than expected. But everyone is taking a bagged lunch, so you're free until supper." He looked directly at Sara. "The park is off-limits to you. You are not to go trekking, prospecting, digging, getting lost, getting injured, or in any way disturbing anyone's peace of mind within park boundaries. Do you hear me?"

Dave rolled his eyes.

"Yeah, yeah, I heard you the first five times," Sara said, but only after Thomas was out of earshot. To Dave, she said, "So what are your plans when we've finished here? Would you like to accompany me?"

"Well, yeah, but where are you going? I mean, I'm all for ignoring Thomas. I do it all the time. But don't you think it's just a little soon to be flaunting the rules? Personally, I always wait at least a day."

"I have no intention of flaunting any rules."

Dave raised an eyebrow.

"Have you any idea how much that makes you look like Thomas?"

He quickly lowered it.

"I could be mistaken," Dave said, "but I thought I heard something about no digging, prospecting, trekking, raising hell or having fun within the park boundaries."

"You did. But that doesn't mean that Thomas wants me to just hang around here twiddling my thumbs."

The eyebrow went up again.

"Okay, maybe he does want that," Sara admitted, "but I'm sure that he doesn't expect it."

"Can't argue with that logic," Dave responded with a grin. "Where are we going, then, since we can't go anywhere?"

"He doesn't want us going anywhere within the park, but he didn't say we couldn't go canoeing outside of the park."

They finished the dishes and headed down to the river. Sara took the stern.

"Anywhere in particular you want to go?" Dave turned around to look at her.

"Let's head south." She wanted to get a quick look at the shoreline southeast of the park's boundaries. She didn't plan to be out too long, because the water was choppy and a fine mist was being carried on the breeze.

Sara saw what she'd hoped to see at their destination. They turned and paddled back quickly. Once their gear was put away, she announced that she planned to go out again the next day. "You're welcome if you want to come."

By midafternoon it was raining heavily and most of the team was gathered in the dining tent. When someone mentioned starting a fire, Patrick suggested that maybe they should do something else for the afternoon.

"It's only supposed to rain for a few hours, but we'll have to wait for things to dry out, so we won't be going back into the field today. Why don't we go to the summer fair in Millicent? We can have supper there."

"Good idea. Who all wants to go?" Thomas said.

Within an hour, they had loaded themselves into the Jeeps and were on their way to Millicent.

The rain had stopped altogether by the time they parked in Millicent. Little patches of blue were beginning to peek through the cloud cover.

"Looks like it's beginning to clear." Thomas fell into step with Sara.

"I hope so," she said. "I'm starting to find all this greyness a bit depressing. Whatever happened to 'Sunny Alberta'?"

"It's just a really weird year." Mike said.

Sara realized she was excited as she stepped through the snow fence into the huge field. She hadn't been to a small country fair for a long time. She started singing along with the band that was playing Murray McLaughlin's "The Farmer's Song". Her stomach growled as the aroma of fried onion rings and hamburgers and popcorn wafted through the air. She could see animal pens and a games area and she immediately decided that she would have to participate in the minnow races.

Love in the Age of Dinosaurs

The members of the team all headed off in different directions. Some were enticed by the food, some wanted to see the animals, and others were interested in bingo and horseshoes.

"Why don't we just meander our way through all the stalls, and then get something to eat?" Sara suggested to Sam and Laura.

"Sounds good to me," said Laura.

"And later we can try our luck at bingo." Sam sounded as if she was ready to have a good time.

They started with the animal pens. A boy who raised rabbits let them hold them and feed them alfalfa. Sam stopped to scratch a lamb, and Laura snorted at an enormous white sow.

After the animals, they went to the crafts show where woodworkers were selling furniture and carvings, some very beautiful and all very expensive. When Sam and Laura went to look at the wooden lawn furniture, Sara lagged, her attention caught by a display of cedar boxes and pine toys, key chains, butterflies, and whirligigs in the shapes of blue jays and bluebirds and bohemian waxwings.

"It'll be hard to choose anything from among these gorgeous things."

The woodworker reached under his table. He pulled out an eighteen-inch cedar wind spinner. "Bin waitin' for just the right customer for this one. It's the last one I have."

Captivated, Sara said, "How much is it?"

"Well, it was gonna be thirty dollars but for you I'll make it twenty-five."

Thoroughly charmed, Sara decided to buy it. "Would you be able to hold it for me until the end of the day?"

She caught up with Laura and Sam at a jumble table that had all kinds of second-hand goods for sale. All three of them sifted through the piles and pointed out unusual items to each other, but Sara didn't see anything she liked as well as the wind spinner.

Sam and Laura wanted to play bingo, so Sara went alone to the minnow races. Patrick and Dave were there, so she joined them. "That's mine, second fish from the right." She handed a loonie to the starter. "He looks young, but I predict a long and glorious career for him. His name is Charles Sternberg, and he's willing to face in friendly fashion the most formidable of foes. He's going to win big for me."

Patrick laughed. "I'll go for Lawrence Lambe on the far right. He looks a little more fragile, but he'll be a steady and erstwhile competitor and attack the job before him with a professional attitude."

"Who are these guys? Palaeontologists? Well then, I choose George Dawson on the left. He's a little stunted, but I'm sure he's a brilliant, well-rounded, artsy kind of competitor. His swimming is undoubtedly poetry in motion."

"That leaves an empty lane," Sara said. "Could I choose a second fish?"

"Certainly not." Thomas appeared out of nowhere. "That's my guy, Barnum Brown."

Sara and Patrick groaned.

Thomas merely grinned. "This dashing fellow is about to make my fortune for me. I expect to clean up here."

And he did. They played ten times, using different fish but the same names, and each time Thomas's choice won the race.

As he collected his winnings, Thomas said, "To show my magnanimity, I'll treat everyone to a slice of pie."

After they had eaten their pie, they separated once again. Patrick and Dave went off to look at old farm machinery. Sara

Love in the Age of Dinosaurs

and Thomas wandered through the exhibits. One room was filled with an amazing number and variety of colourful quilts. Another housed paintings by local artists, including artwork by students.

"I like this one." Sara pointed to a grade three student's rendering of a scarecrow in a cabbage field. Next, her attention was caught by an abstract mauve and blue mountain scene with straight-edged mountain sides that hinted at a cubist style. "Pretty unusual for grade four."

Thomas pulled her over to his favourite, an abstract blue and green finger painting. After that, he didn't let go of her hand. They wandered among stalls displaying stained glass, pottery, woven goods, and various handmade sewn goods. She couldn't remember a time when she had felt more relaxed or happy. *But then, when he's not reaming me out, Thomas always has that effect on me.*

The world was a different place when she was with him. All her cares and worries just seemed to vanish, and the good things in life seemed bigger and brighter. When they passed the wooden ornament table again, Sara stopped to pick up the spinner.

"Like it?" asked Thomas.

"Yes, I'm buying it," Sara replied. "It'll be my souvenir of how I spent the summer."

"Don't buy it," Thomas said suddenly.

"Why not?" asked Sara. "Don't you think I should have a souvenir of the summer?"

"I do," Thomas replied. "And that's why I want to buy it for you."

Sara wasn't sure, but Thomas pointed out that he was still feeling quite flush with all of the winnings from his afternoon at the races. So Sara smiled and accepted his gift.

They all came together for supper, which they ate to the music of local bands. Afterward, Sara was going to ride with Mike, Alan, and Geoff, but Thomas grabbed her around the waist and pulled her into his Jeep.

"What if I don't want to ride with you?" Sara said, as they waited for Dave and Sam.

"I hope you're not still sore about losing to Barnum Brown. There's no changing history, you know," Thomas said with a smile. "Besides, for all its intensity, the rivalry between Sternberg and Brown was a friendly one."

"And he did provide me with a nice new wind spinner."

"What are you going to do with it, Sara?"

"I want to take it out to the lake." She hesitated a fraction of a second, and then added, "I still own the family cabin. I haven't been there for years—ever since the accident—but I'm thinking that I might like to go there sometime."

"Good idea." Thomas was about to say more, but Dave and Sam piled into the back seat, and he held his thoughts. He shared a smile with Sara, though.

Thomas was gratified that Sara had said so much. She was slowly becoming less reticent about her painful past. But this was the first time she had volunteered information that he hadn't asked for.

He looked in the rear view mirror when Sam said, "Look what I got!" She was holding up a cedar wind spinner.

"That's the same as mine," Sara said. "Where did you get it?"

"From a guy in a Blue Jays baseball cap at the table with a green and white cloth."

"How much did you pay for it?" Thomas couldn't resist asking.

"I got a deal. Regular price is thirty dollars, but he said..."

"For you I'll make it twenty-five," Sara said in unison with her.

Sam started to laugh. "And was yours also the last in stock?"

"Of course. Not that I think he was stringing me along or anything. I'm sure he just hadn't gotten around to updating his inventory. It must be terribly difficult to keep an accurate count when spinners are constantly cloning themselves under the table."

When they reached the camp, Thomas asked Sara if she'd like to go for a walk before bed. "Let's stop by my office first. I don't want to forget the files for the funding meeting, so I'll pack them tonight."

Patrick was just hanging up the phone when they entered. He wore a puzzled frown. "Well, that's odd."

"What's odd?" Thomas pulled some dossiers from the filing cabinet.

"I just picked up a message from Jay Sanders."

"From PAIN?"

"Yeah. He'll be arriving with a government official in three days. They want to inspect the area prior to the final allocation of funds. He said it's mostly a formality, but he's looking forward to seeing what we're doing."

"You're right. That is very odd. They only send out inspectors for grants in excess of five hundred thousand dollars. And we only applied for five hundred thousand. Did he say anything else?"

"No, that was it."

Thomas considered the timing. "I'll still be in Calgary when he arrives, which means that you'll have to show him around by yourself."

"No problem. I'm happy to give him a tour. I'm just puzzled about why he's coming."

"I'm sure I'll find out more at the conference. It will probably turn out to be an error. It certainly wouldn't be the first time. Except Jay usually knows what he's doing."

"There has to be some other explanation, then," Patrick said.

"If it's not their error, then I guess it's ours. But we went over that file so many times I find it hard to believe that we made a mistake." He grinned suddenly. "Sure you're not holding out on me, Pat? You didn't alter the application without telling me?"

"If it was altered, then we have a ghostwriter on the premises. The last time I saw the file was with you."

"Well, I'm sure it will all come clear in the end. I'll let you know as soon as I find out what's going on."

chapter

TWENTY-TWO

Sara did not sleep well that night. *I shouldn't have gone on that walk with Thomas. Not that we did much walking. Still, it was way too late. And I wanted to explain what I did to that application, but he didn't want to talk either.*

Sara jumped up. *I'm going to tell him before he leaves for Calgary. Then he'll understand what's going on and can plan for it.* A nasty little voice at the back of her mind pointed out that Thomas ought to have known a lot sooner, and now he had no time to plan for anything.

You knew when you altered that application that you were taunting a tiger.

In the dining tent, she silently planned what she was going to say to Thomas about the funding application. She became so engrossed in how she'd convince him she had acted for the best, that breakfast was nearly over before she noticed he hadn't put in an appearance. "Have you seen Thomas?" she asked Dave.

"Didn't he tell you? He wanted to get a very early start, so he decided to skip breakfast. He must have left just about the time we started cooking."

"Oh no! I really needed to talk to him about something."

Dave raised an eyebrow. "Something good or something not-so-good?"

She chewed her lower lip.

"Again? Wow! Do you have a death wish or what?"

"Well, I don't know for sure it's going to upset him," Sara said in self-defense. "There's a slight possibility that he won't be bothered at all..."

Dave straddled a chair and rested his arms on the back. "I've got to hand it to you, Sara. Before you came along, I was the only one who ever upset Thomas. And it's taken me my whole life and untold effort to learn how to do it. And of course, I like to think I have some small talent for it." He pantomimed a bow.

"But you're a natural! You've had him off balance from the moment you two met. Effortlessly. Do you know what that means?"

Bemused, Sara shook her head.

"It means that together, there's no end to the ways we can drive him crazy!"

For the first time that morning, Sara laughed. "And why, pray tell, do we want to drive him crazy?"

"Nothing as frivolous as 'want', Sara." He shook a finger sternly. "It's our bounden duty."

"Our bounden duty?"

"How else are we going to keep him from developing a swelled head? From the time he was a small boy, Thomas has shown disturbing signs of being tainted with natural leadership qualities. Those unfortunate genes, combined with an unhealthy environment in which everyone kowtows to him like he's the Grand Pooh Bah of Palaeontology, can only lead him to a bad end. Let's face it, Thomas is insufferable and he's modest. Can you imagine what he'll be like if he becomes arrogant?"

Sara wiped her eyes. "You should not be making me laugh. It's just possible that I could be in serious trouble when he gets back."

"Well, what's he going to do? He's already demoted you to the kitchen."

"There are worse things than being in the kitchen."

"Absolutely," Dave said, "but you've already been out digging for dinosaurs. It certainly doesn't get any worse than that."

"What if he fires me?"

"He's not going to fire you," Dave said with complete assurance.

"You know that?"

"Of course I know that."

"How?"

"Because Thomas will take everything into account. Essentially, he is very fair."

"He wouldn't consider it fair to sack me?"

"Of course not."

"Because I've given him so much of my time and energy and expertise."

"Not exactly. It's more that if he let you go, he wouldn't be able to repay you in full for all the worry and pain you've caused him."

Sara stared open mouthed at Dave.

Dave shrugged. "Like I said, he's fair." He stood and set the chair aside. "Look, I know how you feel. You know you are in for it big time. You regret what you did. Or at least the getting caught part. And you know that no matter how sincerely you apologise or how cravenly you grovel, you can't escape what is coming to you. Right?"

"Yeah. Right."

"Right. Then there's only one sensible thing to do."

"Lie low and completely toe the line until he gets back," Sara concluded.

Dave gave her a pained look. "Well, actually, my philosophy has always been more along the lines of 'in for a penny, in for a pound'. So I suggest you go and break as many rules as you possibly can in as many ways as you can possibly devise. After all, if you're going to die an ignominious death, you can at least take some pride in deserving it."

Sara happened to look past Dave just then. Barney had just about completed a successful raid. He was headed for the door with a loaf of bread in his mouth. As soon as Dave yelled, he started to run.

Dave managed to grab one end of the loaf, but the dog got away with the other half. "That's the third time this week that he's managed to do that." Dave sounded completely disgusted. "The day before yesterday he got a pound of bacon, too. So there's your role model, Sara. Talk about total unswerving commitment

Love in the Age of Dinosaurs

to a life of crime. Time and again he continues with his thieving ways. And he never repents. And who is better loved of Thomas?"

Dave continued regaling Sara with tales of Barney's criminal activities. "He isn't even fazed by the fact that he could die from eating dark chocolate. A whole box of semi-sweet cooking chocolate downed in one gulp. And when I found the mutilated box, he wagged his tail and smiled at me!"

The dishes done, Dave and Sara headed to the river. Sara had suggested they go to the area southeast of the park's boundary and hike around a bit. As they were launching the canoe, Barney appeared, wagging his tail and sniffing the paddles. He cocked his head as Sara settled herself in the bow seat.

"Come on!" Sara tried to persuade him onto the canoe, but he just sat there.

As they started away from the shore, Barney hung his head and looked so forlorn that they paddled back. When Sara called this time, he waded through the shallow water and, with Sara's help, clambered in.

Once in, Barney appeared to be frightened by the rocking of the canoe and he tried to climb onto Sara's lap. The canoe started to tip, but Dave counterbalanced by leaning the other way. Finally, Barney hopped into the middle and stretched out under the yoke. He was the first to hop out when they landed on the Crown land that Thomas was hoping would someday be a part of the park.

"Should we be worried about trespassing?" Dave said, as they were pulling the canoe higher on the bank.

"I don't think so. Thomas's team has permission to be here, and we're part of the team, aren't we?"

Dave's eyebrow went up.

"What? You're the cook. In my book, that makes you the most important member of the team. And yes, I might be suspended, but I haven't yet been told that I'm no longer on the team." *That's probably coming when Thomas finds out about the funding application.*

"Just one teensy little question. Which one of us is going to explain that to Thomas if we happen to get caught?"

"I can't believe you're behaving this way." Sara put her hands on her hips. "Whatever happened to Dave the daring, Dave the happy-go-lucky-let-the-chips-fall-where-they-may, carefree and reckless Dave?"

"Sorry." Dave gave his head a shake. "Gosh. I think Thomas's worst prediction about my future just came true." He shivered. "Wow! Talk about unnerving experiences!"

"What are you talking about?"

"Thomas is always saying that one of these days I am going to learn to think before I act. And just now, totally out of the blue, the most unpleasant thoughts about the possible consequences of our behaviour flashed through my mind. Don't know what came over me. For a whole minute there, I came dangerously close to seeing things from his point of view."

"You're scared!" Sara accused. "Why?"

"It does sound a bit like that, doesn't it?" Dave sounded astonished. "I can't think why. I'm only interfering in Thomas's livelihood in ways that could have negative repercussions for him on a personal and professional level. The fall-out from that will surely be disastrous for you and me, but that is no reason for an attack of the jitters."

"You are being a ninny! We are not interfering in Thomas's livelihood. We already did that when we altered that funding application form. Today we're just going to take a look around. How could that possibly have a negative effect on anyone?"

"So said the hang glider when he harnessed himself to a tornado instead of an aeroplane," Dave replied. "So busy enjoying the wind beneath his wings, he sort of overlooked the little bits of destruction wherever they touched down."

"Maybe you should just wait by the canoe," Sara said.

Dave grinned. "Don't worry, I'm not about to disintegrate to the point where I actually start acting responsibly. I haven't lost sight of our noble objective, which is to infuriate Thomas."

"We are not aiming to infuriate Thomas," Sara said. "We are aiming to help Thomas."

"Help him how?"

She explained what she was looking for in this area. She also explained why.

Dave whistled. "You're not exactly an underachiever, are you, Sara?"

"So are you going to help or what?"

"I will do everything I can to help. I, too, desire to help Thomas. And I truly believe that we will be helping Thomas. There's just one little thing you should be aware of."

"What?"

"Sooner or later—probably sooner than later—Thomas is going to understand that we are helping him."

"And?"

"And it is probably going to infuriate him."

They didn't find anything that day, but Sara familiarised herself with the lay of the land and the soils and rock formations, so she had some ideas for the next day. They returned to camp just in time to cook supper.

As they worked, people began to drift in. Since supper was not yet ready, some headed for the stream or the hot showers, some to their tents. Patrick announced that he was going over to the office to make his daily phone call to Mary.

He returned, looking worried, just as supper was being served.

"What's wrong, Patrick?" Sara said. "Is Mary all right?"

"No, she's not. She's having difficulty breathing and some terrible headaches."

"What does the doctor say?"

"She's already been admitted to the hospital. The doctor wants to see both of us tonight. I wanted to leave right away, but Mary insisted that I eat first. So I'm going right after supper." He sipped his drink.

"I've already spoken to Thomas. I told him I'll be back in time to show Jay around the day after tomorrow."

"Did Thomas say anything else?" Sara couldn't resist asking.

"Yeah. He'll try to cut out early and be back in time to help give Jay the tour. We didn't have time to talk about anything else." He looked at his watch. "I've got to get going. See you tomorrow."

"Give Mary my best. I hope to see her soon."

"Will do." Patrick left, nearly running.

chapter TWENTY-THREE

The next morning the sky was overcast and the air muggy. Rain had fallen overnight and Sara had to skirt puddles on her way to the dining tent.

"What an oppressive atmosphere," she said to Dave as they washed up after breakfast.

"Yeah," agreed Dave. "The air is wrapped around me like an unwanted blanket I can't shake off."

"We're in for another electrical storm," Geoff remarked, as he picked up a lunch bag. "We'll have...Hey, who's that?"

Three men had gotten out of a dark-coloured sedan and were walking up the lane. They all wore jackets, jeans, and hiking boots, and one carried a backpack and a macintosh.

"Oh. My. Goodness." Sara fumbled behind her back with the apron strings. "It can't be. They're a day early."

She heard Geoff say, "Who..." as she left the dining tent and walked out to greet the newcomers.

"Sara Wickham, you gorgeous girl!" The tall, fair-haired man caught Sara in a bear hug and lifted her off her feet.

"It's good to see you, too, Jay." She grinned from ear to ear.

He set her down, but kept his arm across her shoulders. "Sara, meet Terence Clark, assistant deputy minister with a special portfolio relating to parks. Terence, Sara Wickham, palaeontologist extraordinaire. And you know Adrian, of course."

Sara held out her hand to Terence, but only nodded curtly to Adrian. "Pleased to meet you, Terence. Hi, Adrian. How are you? Maybe we all should sit down in the field office and discuss—"

"That won't be necessary," Jay said. "We'd like to get out and take a look around before the weather gets nasty. Terence has a very busy schedule and has only been able to clear this one day for a field trip. I just phoned Thomas and told him about the change of plans. He said he couldn't be here until tomorrow, but gave me a list of several people here who could show us around." Placing his hands on Sara's shoulders, he turned her to face him. "Funny that he didn't mention you, Sara."

Sara shrugged. "Maybe he doesn't know that we know each other."

Love in the Age of Dinosaurs

"But still..." Jay persisted, obviously unwilling to drop the issue. "He told me that Patrick is at the hospital with Mary, and he mentioned several technicians and graduate students. Yet he neglected to mention that one of palaeontology's rising stars is available to give guided tours."

Sara shrugged again. "Well, you know how it is. You're taken by surprise and you start listing people and sometimes you leave out a few names."

"Only one name," said Jay. "Yours."

Sara gritted her teeth. "Well, I'm sure I can't explain it. You'll have to ask Thomas."

Jay pursed his lips thoughtfully, but said no more. Geoff and Dave had come out to meet the newcomers and they began discussing where to go.

Geoff gave Sara a very sharp look when she suggested that Geoff take Adrian in one direction while she took Jay, and possibly Terence, in another.

"Could you excuse us for just a moment?" Geoff said. "Sara and I just need to discuss something quickly."

When he got her alone, he demanded, "What in blazes do you think you're doing? You know what Thomas said. You're not supposed to leave the kitchen."

"Well, what option do we have?" Sara retorted. "Jay expects me to show him around. I can't just say, 'Oh, okay. There's the camp stove, that's the breadbox, and here's where we pile the firewood.' Come on, Geoff. It's in our best interest if we spread out and show them some different things.

"You can show Adrian the areas we've been working in this summer and what's been earmarked for the next field season. I'll show Jay some other interesting things. Terence can choose where he wants to go. Then they can compare notes and make a more informed decision."

Geoff finally agreed, although he was clearly not very happy about it. He went to put supplies in the Jeep.

Terence opted to accompany Sara and Jay.

"Do you know where they're going or how they're getting there?" Adrian asked Terence. "Or do they know themselves?" He bestowed a disparaging look upon both Sara and Jay.

"Of course I know," Sara replied coolly. "We're taking the canoe over to an area just southeast of the current park's boundaries. I have a strong hunch that what we find there will impress even a hardened soul like yours, Adrian."

"It's your hunches that have hardened my soul, Sara," Adrian said. "Couldn't whatever is supposedly waiting there to impress us all wait until the weather improves? It hardly seems appropriate to be going out in a canoe when an electrical storm is forecast."

"The storm isn't supposed to hit until mid-afternoon. We'll be back long before that." Sara imbued her voice with confidence. "We'll be fine. Now why don't you pack up all your little worries and head off with Geoff? He's waiting, safely and patiently, in the Jeep."

Adrian regarded Sara for a long, drawn-out moment. "I hope you know what you are doing, but since I am almost certain that you do not, you'd better take the first aid kit and this spare mac." He rummaged through his rucksack and pulled out the kit and shoved it into Sara's hands. He gave Jay the spare raincoat. "You can return them to me when I see you at the hospital." He turned and walked away.

"Well, that's a relief," Jay said cheerfully. "I was hoping you'd get rid of him quickly and you didn't disappoint."

Love in the Age of Dinosaurs

"Whatever possessed you to bring him along? You know what he's like in the field."

"Wasn't my idea," Jay said. "Boss's orders."

As they carried the canoe to the water, Terence said, "So what is our plan for this morning?"

Jay snickered. "Yeah, Sara. What do you plan to do to us today?"

She shot him a glare. "Don't you start with me, Dr. Sanders. I know what you're thinking and you know very well it wasn't my fault."

"This sounds interesting." Terence looked from one to the other.

"Oh, Sara is nothing if not interesting." Jay was grinning widely. "We've spent a lot of time doing interesting field work together. The last time I went fossil hunting with Sara, we ended up going to a hospital to view a lot of very interesting bone fractures."

"Were you using a CT scanner to look at broken dinosaur bones?" said Terence, with interest.

"Yeah, but that came later. They used ordinary x-rays for ours. Sara needed a cast on her wrist and I ended up with one on my thumb and one on my leg."

"We don't need to bore Terence with a lot of tired old reminiscences," Sara said.

"Then there was the time we got caught in that interesting hailstorm." Jay threw a laughing look her way. "I had so many interesting pockmarks on my arms that people started asking me if I'd had smallpox."

"A silly question if ever there was one. Smallpox has long been eradicated."

"Yeah, and a lot more easily than those scars I carried for so long," Jay said. "And then there was that most interesting experience we had with vandals the time—"

"Do you want to sit in the middle," Sara said, "or do you want to paddle?"

The men opted to paddle, so Sara sat in the middle and directed them where to land. On the way, she explained many of the landscape features they would see and described some of the finds that had already been made in the area. By the time they were beaching the canoe, a light rain was falling. "I'm sorry, Terence, but in view of the weather, I think maybe we should postpone our tour of this area for another day," she said.

"I've only got today," Terence replied. "If you don't mind getting a bit wet, I'd rather continue."

"No, I don't mind getting a bit wet. I thought you might." She wondered if a little of Thomas was rubbing off on her. She felt responsible for the welfare of the men, and her inclination was to return to the camp to wait out the inclement weather.

"Shall we head over to those coulees?" Jay indicated an area on the map. "They look promising."

"Well, actually, I think we should go this way." Sara pointed in the opposite direction. "I have a hunch—"

"Oh no." Jay groaned. "Not one of your hunches, Sara. That can only mean we'll be facing great danger or great discomfort or a great deal of both." To Terence he said, "The second last time I was prospecting with Sara, she had one of her hunches, and we almost died on the edge of a—"

"That was when we were very young."

"Well, I was talking to Andrew Turner just last week, and he claimed that—"

Love in the Age of Dinosaurs

Sara said to Terence, "It's going to be a bit of a hike. It's already past noon. It's starting to rain, and the weather is supposed to worsen. Are you absolutely sure that you can't come back another day?"

Terence opted to continue, so they headed off. The soil was already slick from the rains the previous night, and they were all muddy by the time they reached the area Sara had the hunch about. Her left knee was throbbing because she had twisted it the last time she fell.

They were also drenched. The wind had picked up and was dashing the cold rain against their bodies. Shivering, they huddled together at the base of a small hill.

"Now I'm beginning to remember why I left the field and took an office job." Jay's teeth chattered as he spoke.

"Were you in the field for a long time?" Terence said. "It sounds like you've had a lot of extraordinary experiences."

"Oh yes, I did. But that was all just in one season working with Sara. Then she left, thankfully before I perished from all the interesting experiences we were having." He laughed and put his arm around her. "That last time, I was in the hospital for a week and the doctors prescribed a strong dose of boring, safe, non-life-threatening experiences. In short, they ordered me to stop working with Sara."

"Don't listen to him. Sometimes, we might have gotten a little more than we bargained for, but I think it's exaggerating to say that our lives were ever truly endangered. Besides, both of us made full recoveries from any injuries due to random acts of nature."

Sara was miserably aware that they were all soaked to the skin. If anything, the rain was falling harder, and the clouds were blacker. She could hear thunder rumbling in the distance.

Sorcha Lang

"I think we should go back. But since we're here already, I want to run up this hill and take a quick look at the mudstone. I'll just be a few minutes. You can wait here or start back."

"No, we'll come," Jay said. "That's what we're here for."

Sara led the way. At the top she turned to make sure the men were following and her foot slipped. She rolled head over heels down the other side. On the way, her left hand struck a sharp rock and was gashed deeply.

Jay, who had reached forward to grab her, also lost his footing and came sliding down behind her. He landed hard.

Terence half slid, half skidded down the hill behind them.

Before Terence could speak, Sara pointed speechlessly at something sticking out of the ground between her and Jay.

Jay, whose face was ashen, turned to look and his eyes widened. He grinned briefly before he grimaced with pain.

"What is it?" Terence said.

"Broken wrist, I think." Jay said.

chapter

TWENTY-FOUR

"A broken wrist?" repeated Thomas.

"Yes." Andrew said. "And Sara was lucky. Jay broke his thumb and his leg."

"Who?" The word shot out of his mouth like a bullet. Thomas stopped smiling.

Andrew paused with his wineglass halfway to his mouth. Thomas had run into him at the wine and cheese reception hosted by the Palaeontology and Archaeology Institute. They had been trading stories about fieldwork. Thomas had laughed heartily as Andrew recounted several of his staff's harrowing experiences. But when Andrew mentioned their names, he stopped laughing.

"Sara Wickham and Jay Sanders," Andrew repeated. "They were prone to having interesting adventures."

"That figures." Thomas sipped his wine. "So what happened next?"

"Well, Adrian was okay, albeit badly bruised, so after splinting them, he walked out alone to get help. The paramedics had to carry Jay on a stretcher for about three kilometres."

"And Sara?"

"Oh, she walked. As soon as she got her cast, I put her on the next available plane and sent her home. The expedition was at an end anyway. I followed her two days later. That gave me time to compose what I wanted to say to her. I practised it on Jay first."

"And no doubt they listened attentively and promised never to do such a thing again," Thomas said.

"Well, Jay did. He was suitably sobered. When he recovered, he was seconded to PAIN. I don't think he's been on an expedition since. Too bad, actually. Like Sara, he's brilliant at prospecting."

"Well, he's having a tour of Dinosaur Provincial Park today. Maybe that will inspire him to return to fieldwork."

"Maybe." Andrew chuckled. "Good thing Sara's not there. Together, they were a formidable team. But they took too many risks. That's why I always sent Adrian along. For a bit of common sense."

Thomas choked on a sip of wine. He started to say that Sara *was* at Dinosaur Provincial Park, but Andrew was still talking.

Love in the Age of Dinosaurs

"Speaking of Sara, I need to ask Patrick if he's heard from her. She seems to have disappeared off the face of the earth. No one knows where she is. When I get my hands on her, I'll—"

"Wring her lovely long neck?" Thomas suggested. On the verge of revealing Sara's whereabouts to Andrew, Thomas hesitated and swallowed his words. "Why don't you know where Sara is? Why would she just disappear?"

As Andrew explained, Thomas's stomach clenched. He forced himself to inhale slowly and deeply.

"Are you telling me that you actually fired Sara to force her to take a holiday?"

"Just temporarily," Andrew was quick to explain. "I don't want to lose her. But she has worked every single day for at least three years. She's exhausted and reckless, a lethal combination if ever there was one. She needs some time off to rest before she has a serious accident or illness. So I confiscated all of her equipment and told her that if she so much as reads the word 'dinosaur' in a comic book, there will be hell to pay when she gets back. Then I sent her on a three-month holiday." He seemed to swell with satisfaction.

"Drastic measures, I admit, but I'm pretty sure I finally got through to her."

Thomas raised an eyebrow. "You're sure, are you?"

"You sound sceptical, Tom. Do you know something I don't?"

"Apparently not," Thomas said. "In all honesty, at this moment I have to say I really don't know much about Sara Wickham at all."

"I wasn't aware that you two had even met."

"Oh, ours is a fairly recent acquaintanceship." Thomas was deliberately vague. "We have mutual friends and we've been at some of the same sites and social gatherings."

"And it's impossible not to notice Sara," Andrew said.

Thomas had to agree. "She's pretty amazing. She's smart, beautiful, kind, funny, perceptive, talented, generous, good company…"

"I thought you said you didn't know her very well," Andrew said with a grin. "That's a long string of compliments. But then, everyone seems to fall for her."

Thomas gave him a sharp look. "You too?"

"Ours is a platonic relationship. As far as I know, Sara's not romantically involved with anyone. Just as well, because she's always working, and doesn't really have time for a relationship."

So there was a positive side to Sara's work habits after all. "A romantic entanglement while she's trying to establish her career is the very last thing Sara needs."

Unless it's with me.

He strongly doubted that any of Sara's male friends were deserving of her, and he'd no intention of letting them get close enough for her to decide otherwise.

I'm probably not deserving of her either, but I've never wanted anyone the way I want her.

Their conversation was interrupted by someone calling their names. Aaron Baker joined them. He had his hands full with a large plate of canapés and a stack of files tucked precariously under one arm. "Thomas. Andrew. Good to see you. I've been looking for you all day."

"Only a workaholic arrives at a party with his arms full of files." Andrew helped Aaron set the files on a nearby table.

Love in the Age of Dinosaurs

"Our funding allocation meeting just ended." Aaron took back the plate Thomas had rescued. "I thought the reception would be over by the time I dropped these in my room and came back."

"So what tidings do you bring?" Thomas said.

"Good tidings." Aaron nodded vigorously. "Very good tidings." He stuffed a canapé in his mouth and swallowed it quickly.

"You've each been awarded the million in funding that you requested for next year, Congratulations! You were the only two who applied for the available discretionary funds. That category is being eliminated and we had to use up the money, so they split it between you. Your projects will have to pass the inspections, but those are just formalities, so I'm sure you've got the money."

Andrew grinned widely. "Great news!" He said to Thomas, "You know, Sara told me we were eligible for those funds and I didn't believe her. But I learned a long time ago to trust her judgement on these things. She's been doing all of my funding applications for the last two years. So I just told her to go ahead and do as she saw fit." He raised his glass to clink with Aaron's.

Aaron gave Thomas a curious look. "What's the matter, Tom? Doesn't an extra half-million excite you?"

"It would," Thomas said, "if I didn't think you were mistaken."

Aaron raised his brows. "What do you mean? I participated in the allocations. There's no error."

"There has to be. I didn't apply for those discretionary funds. Someone has made a serious mistake."

"It wasn't us. But let's check. I have all the applications right here." He sorted through his files. "Here it is. Let's take a look." He scanned the sheets quickly and handed one to Thomas.

Thomas read the form with disbelief. The discretionary funds category was neatly filled in with block capitals. It was not his printing; nor was it Patrick's. He remembered misplacing the file, looking for the file. Then he remembered who had found the file.

For a moment, he was speechless. "I guess you're right," he managed at last. "I guess in the rush at the last minute, I lost track of all the decisions that were being made." With an effort, he plastered a big smile on his face. "That's great, that's just great."

He remained with the others for another quarter of an hour, and then excused himself and returned to his room. He wanted to talk to Sara. He wanted to call Patrick. He wanted to celebrate the fact that Sara had gotten them extra funding.

He failed miserably at all three. He had to leave a message at the camp when no one picked up. He had to leave a voice mail message for Patrick. And to his dismay, Thomas realised that his anger with Sara was much, much greater than his happiness at what she had achieved.

chapter

TWENTY-FIVE

Jay's wrist was already discoloured and beginning to swell. "You're probably right," Terence said when he'd examined it. "It certainly looks like it's broken."

"There are probably some splints in Adrian's first aid kit. He always makes sure he has absolutely everything anyone could possibly use in any contingency."

Terence found the splints and, with Sara's help and instructions, managed to immobilise Jay's wrist. Jay no longer looked like he was about to faint, but he was still very pale and was obviously still in some discomfort.

Sara, meanwhile, had wound a bandage around her palm. "Just a scratch," she said quickly, at Terence's worried expression. "Nothing to worry about. I'll be fine."

She continued to apply direct pressure, but still blood seeped through the bandage. Finally, she allowed Terence to tape some pads tightly to her palm and wind more gauze over them.

Terence found a packet of painkillers, which he opened and handed to Jay. A few minutes later Sara reached over and surreptitiously took one for herself. But all her concern was for Jay.

She was worried about keeping him as warm and dry as possible, and insisted he wear the macintosh Adrian had provided. She rummaged through the first aid kit. "Aha! Good old Adrian." She held up two disposable foot warmers. She activated them and put them inside the macintosh, close to his body.

"This rain is bound to slacken off before too long. When it does, we'll be able to move and that will warm us up. In the meantime we should just huddle together."

The next few hours were about the most miserable Sara had ever spent. The rain finally did let up marginally, but by then an electrical storm was upon them. They separated, and crouched low, arms wrapped around their heads. All around them, the lightning and the thunder flashed and roared in the most severe storm of the summer.

There had been a time in the not-too-distant past when life held so little appeal for Sara that she couldn't be bothered with basic safety precautions. But now that it was truly threatened, her future seemed full of endless possibility.

She thought about Patrick and Mary and the new life they were bringing into the world, about Dave and his cheerful optimism, Thomas and how he had wanted to keep her safe. She thought about the joy she felt when she was with him. She decided that if she did survive this encounter with the elements, she was never, ever, going to get into this kind of situation again. *I wonder if PAIN has any openings available.*

Eventually, the storm moved on. By the time the rain had diminished sufficiently for them to move, night had fallen. Heavy clouds completely blotted out the moon and the stars. They decided to remain where they were until the first light, rather than take the chance of incurring further injury by stumbling around blindly in the dark.

At first their conversation meandered from topic to topic, but eventually the words dried up and they became quiet.

Sara hunkered down in her cocoon of misery. From time to time, she emerged and asked the men how they were doing, but she quickly retreated back into silence.

She tried to distract herself from the cold and her empty stomach by thinking about their amazing discovery. Thomas could not fail to be excited by it. However, she had also learned the hard way that Thomas was not easily sidetracked.

If he's angry with me, no discovery, no matter how significant, is going to distract him from that. She thanked her lucky stars that Thomas was far, far away.

When dawn finally arrived, Sara stretched her stiff limbs and painfully stood up. She would give anything to soak in a hot bath for an entire day. When Jay and Terence were ready to go, she automatically reached for her rucksack. When her bandaged palm came into contact with the strap, she barely suppressed a scream. She blinked back tears until the searing pain diminished to an excruciating throb. She grabbed the rucksack with her other hand and, keeping her head down so no one would see the tears she hadn't been able to hold back, muttered, "Okay. Let's go."

Slowly, in order to avoid jarring Jay's wrist as much as possible, they retraced their route. Every ten minutes or so, they stopped to rest. During their third rest stop, a light rain began to fall. With a groan, Sara got to her feet. As she stepped forward, her foot slipped on the greasy soil and she fell heavily onto her hip. She lay looking up at the gray sky for a few seconds, and then her view was blocked by a pair of deep brown eyes and a lolling tongue that began to lick the tears from her cheeks.

"Barney!"

Barney sat back on his haunches and barked excitedly a few times before he put his head back and howled.

Barney's howl reached Dave and Thomas, who were not far behind him.

"That's it, that's Barney's love call!" Dave cried. "He's found them."

A vast sense of relief surged through Thomas. "Let's go!"

Minutes later, he spotted the bedraggled trio. Jay and Terence were sitting upright, and managed to wave. Sara was flat out on the ground and the dog was sitting on top of her. Barney looked over when Thomas called him, but then he turned back to Sara and settled himself more comfortably on her stomach.

By tacit agreement, Dave headed for the two men and Thomas raced over to Sara. He yanked Barney off and started feeling for broken bones. When she assured him she was fine, he helped her sit up. He closed his eyes and hugged her tightly to his chest. "Thank God you're alive," he murmured. He wrapped his jacket around her and then held her close, willing his warmth to seep into her body.

When she stopped shaking, he grasped her shoulders. "Are you sure you're not hurt?"

Love in the Age of Dinosaurs

Sara nodded, even though her hand was throbbing. "Jay is injured. I think his wrist is broken."

"Jay?" In his concern for Sara, he had momentarily forgotten about the men.

He turned his head. They were filthy and sodden. Terence's face was pale and drawn. Jay was clearly in pain. He was standing with Dave's help, but he looked pretty unsteady.

The full implications of the predicament hit Thomas like a load of concrete.

He tightened his grip on Sara as his initial relief morphed into a white-hot anger such as he had never before experienced. "What the hell were you doing out here?"

"I wasn't—I didn't—"

"You didn't what? Think? Care? Plan?" He shook her hard. "When are you going to learn?" He was dimly aware that he was shouting. He didn't care. He felt like shouting.

Tears streamed down Sara's cheeks. She didn't care either. She didn't want Thomas to be kind to her. She had ruined his livelihood. She deserved every bit of his anger.

"Tom."

Thomas gave no sign that he had heard.

"Tom," Dave repeated. He pointed at Jay. "You're needed over there."

Thomas abruptly let go of Sara. Without another word, he stood and walked away.

Dave crouched beside her.

"Are you all right, Sara?" At her nod, he hugged her close. "You don't know how worried we've been. Adrian and Geoff got back yesterday afternoon. We kept expecting you, but you didn't show. That Adrian is not the most optimistic of fellows, is he?"

Sara forced herself to smile briefly. "No, but he wasn't always like that. The more experienced he got, the more jaded his outlook became."

"Yeah, he says so too. *Bitter* experience with you and Jay, was what he called it. It sounded like the two of you drove him completely bonkers when you worked together. Man, you sure took a lot of chances, Sara."

"Do you mean to say that that rat whiled away the time by regaling you with his stories of our fieldwork together?"

"We didn't have anything else to do while we waited for the storm to clear," Dave said. "He's actually a pretty good storyteller. He had most of us howling with laughter even though we were worried sick. Only Thomas never laughed."

"Thomas was there? The whole time?"

"Nope. He got there around midnight."

"And at any time did Adrian express his best wishes for our safe recovery?"

"Not exactly. He said he sincerely hoped that this time you were in so much misery you would have no choice but to change your behaviour."

"He said *that* to Thomas?"

"'Fraid so. Can you walk?"

Sara tucked her injured hand further up her sleeve and nodded.

Thomas walked ahead with Jay and Terence. When they arrived at the river, Geoff and Mike were waiting beside a rowboat fitted with a small outboard motor. Jay and Terence were helped into the boat with Thomas and Barney. Mike and Geoff got into one canoe, leaving the other for Dave and Sara.

"Where did the boat come from?" Sara asked Dave, once she was seated in the bow.

Love in the Age of Dinosaurs

"Ben Stowe."

She tried to pick up a paddle, but her injured hand sent knives of pain up her arm and she quickly dropped it.

"I'll do the paddling. You rest," Dave said.

Adrian had taken charge at the camp. Laura and Sam were cooking and the others had built a roaring bonfire. When Sara and Dave edged close to the fire, Adrian thrust mugs of hot chocolate into their hands. Thomas was already hustling Terence and Jay off to the showers.

"It's more important at the moment to deal with hypothermia than with the wrist," he said to Jay. "Your wrist is already immobilised and you'd probably just have to wait in emergency anyway. So let's get you warm and dry before you go to the hospital. Adrian tells me there is hot soup for you when you're done showering." He didn't even look Sara's way.

Sara watched him wistfully. She sipped her hot chocolate. "Well, Adrian," she said, "you were right as usual. Like always, I screwed up big time. As usual, people are injured. As usual, if it hadn't been for your forethought and first aid kit, we'd have been even worse off than we are. Worst of all, I've infuriated the very person I most want to..." She tried to swallow the lump in her throat.

To her surprise, Adrian put his arm around her. "It's not the end of the world, Sara. Terence and Jay explained what happened. Terence is fine, and Jay's going to be okay as soon as his arm is properly set. You just need a hot shower and some food." He gave her a little shove in the direction of the showers. "Go now."

Adrian's kindness should not have surprised her. In the past, he had always been very calm and supportive during emergencies. Only afterwards, once everyone was okay, did he let loose with his stinging rebukes. She had a feeling that this time he was going to leave the rebuking to Thomas.

Sara sank onto the wooden bench in the empty shower room. She hung her head between her knees, cradling her injured hand against her stomach. Wasn't direct pressure supposed to suppress pain? It wasn't working. She felt like howling, especially when she saw the bloodstains she was leaving all over Thomas's jacket as she struggled to undo it. She never did get it fully unzipped, just let it fall to the floor and stepped out of it. She couldn't do the same with her jeans, and fumbled with each button. She didn't think she'd ever get the knots out of her left bootlaces and she nearly gave up and showered with the boot still on. Finally, fully undressed, she turned the water as hot as it would go and stepped in.

She faced the stream of water and dangled her left arm outside the shower curtain. Twice the soap slipped out of her right hand as she rubbed it across her body and she had to scrabble on the floor for it. She didn't attempt to wash her hair, just rinsed it under the flow of water. Drying herself properly proved impossible and huge wet patches showed through the sweatsuit that she managed to pull on with one hand. Wincing, she wound more gauze around her injury.

When she emerged from the shower room, Sara headed for the field office. It was empty. Jay and Adrian's car was gone. She backtracked to the dining tent.

"They've gone to the hospital in Brooks," Dave said. "Jay seemed a little out of it, but Terence asked why you weren't going with them. Thomas told them he'd bring you along a bit later." Dave looked soberly at Sara. "Have you spoken to Thomas yet?"

"I'm going to now. I need to explain what happened and apologise. If he'll let me."

Love in the Age of Dinosaurs

Dave rubbed his chin. "Uh, Sara, maybe you should give it a little more time. I think he's still feeling kind of—"

"Unhappy?"

"'Homicidal' is the word I think I'm looking for. It might be wise to just steer clear for the next few days."

"I can't do that. I need to sort it out. I can't bear for him to be angry with me. I need to at least tell him that I'm sorry and explain why I...." She turned to walk away. "I'll talk to you later, Dave."

Perhaps Dave was right. How tempting it was to simply keep out of Thomas's way for the next little while. *I just can't do that. I owe him an explanation. And then I need to go to the hospital for stitches.*

She slid her hand out of her sleeve and looked at the soggy bandage. Blood was beginning to seep through the layers, and she didn't dare undo the bandage to look underneath.

She stood uncertainly for a moment in the doorway to Thomas's office. He was on the telephone, assuring someone that Terence was fine and would soon be calling.

Thomas's motions showed his weariness as he hung up the phone. He looked up but didn't say anything.

Sara walked in and said hesitantly, "Thomas, could I talk to you for a minute? I can explain—"

"Oh, spare me, Sara." His face looked drawn and exhausted, but his eyes were smouldering. "I have neither the time nor the energy nor the patience at the moment to listen to your inane excuses, your appalling lies. I hope you are satisfied. You have done more damage here in a single field season than the worst palaeontologists have managed in their entire careers. It'll probably take my whole career to sort out the mess you have created for me."

"I was trying to help you," she whispered.

"Oh, really?" Thomas said in a voice dripping with contempt. "Thank goodness you were *helping*. I hate to think what you would do if you were hindering. Do you always help in such estimable ways?

"You have forged important documents and sabotaged an official inspection, causing calamity for the whole team and injury to the inspectors. You have ruined our chances of receiving funding, scuttled the park border issue, and done everything you can to undermine the team and me. I'm fed up with your antics, I'm fed up with your irresponsibility, and most of all, I'm just plain fed up with you."

Sara froze in shock as the venom in his voice penetrated her mind and her heart. "Thomas, please, I—"

"I don't care to hear what you have to say. It's undoubtedly all lies anyway."

Sara felt the blood drain from her face. "I've never lied to you," she said through stiff lips. "Never."

"No? You said you were free to work here this summer."

"I was free."

"You led me to believe that you had your supervisor's permission." Thomas's tone was flat. "And don't bother to lie about it. I had a long talk with Andrew yesterday."

She stared helplessly. "If you'll just listen, I can explain—"

"No. The only thing I want to hear is the sound of your footsteps as you walk out of here. So why don't you do us both a big favour. Get out of my sight."

Thomas's words hung between them for a moment while Sara stood paralysed. Thomas saw the sick, stricken look that crossed her face in the split second before she turned on her heel and disappeared out the door.

Love in the Age of Dinosaurs

"Sara!" he called, "I didn't mean it! I'm sor—"

He jumped up, knocking his chair over in the process. Ignoring the jangling telephone, he raced after her to the entrance. He flung the door open, started down the steps two at a time and collided with Patrick, who was taking them two at a time in the opposite direction. There was no sign of Sara.

"Sorry, Pat," he muttered as he disentangled himself. "Get the phone, will you? I've got to find Sara."

"I think *you'd* better get that phone," Patrick said, holding on to Thomas's arm. "I'm positive that it's some pretty high-powered people who are wondering what on earth we've done with their employees." He started pushing Thomas back up the steps. "People have been calling me all morning. We've got some heavy-duty explaining to do, and since I don't know what's been going on, I can't do it. *You* have to."

Sara stumbled blindly to her tent. She barely registered the pain in her palm. It had ceased to be a separate hurt. Her heart seemed to have shattered like a firework and each falling shard pierced her so cruelly that she no longer knew where pain began and where it ended. All she could see was Thomas's face. All she could hear were his words repeating themselves over and over in her head. *Get out of my sight. Get out of my sight.*

She found herself in her tent without any recollection of how she had gotten there. In a daze, she threw her few belongings into her pack. Before she left, she paused a moment and looked at the wind spinner Thomas had given her, and then she left it and her tent behind.

Unaware of anyone or anything except the need to distance herself from the camp as quickly and completely as possible, she headed for the main road. Once there, she trekked uphill and out of the park, and reached the prairie rim. When she saw a familiar truck pulling a boat, she stuck out her thumb.

Ben Stowe pulled over. "Hi there, Sara. Need a lift somewhere?"

"Are you going towards Brooks?"

"Hop in. I'm headed that way." He frowned slightly as Sara hefted her bag into the back of the truck, and clambered into the cab. "Isn't that the same bag you came with? Are you leaving?"

"Yeah, I'm leaving," Sara gave him a tired smile. "My season's over and I'm heading out."

"But why isn't anyone giving you a lift?" Ben set the truck in motion.

"Well, the vehicles are all in use. We had a bit of a mishap yesterday. So everyone's pretty busy dealing with all that. I guess they borrowed your boat this morning. Thanks for that."

"Yeah. No worries," Ben said.

Ben glanced over at her. "Hope I'm not prying, Sara, but it seems like a strange way to end your season. Thomas usually has a wrap-up party and he usually invites those of us who live in the area."

Sara managed a wobbly smile. "I don't know Thomas's plans this year. I'm not in them." Her voice had a slight quaver.

Ben looked at her again. "Are you all right?" He leaned closer. "What's wrong with your hand?"

Sara tucked her hand back into her sleeve. "I have a cut, and I think I might need a few stitches. But just drop me wherever, and I'll hitch a ride into Brooks."

"Not bloody likely."

Ben insisted on dropping her right at the emergency entrance. He wanted to come in with her, but Sara finally managed to convince him otherwise.

chapter

TWENTY-SIX

The phone rang for the fourth time since Patrick had arrived in Thomas's office. This time it was the call Thomas had been hoping for.

"Hello, Terence. How is Jay?"

"He's going to be fine. They're putting a cast on now. We should be back first thing tomorrow morning. I've cancelled all my appointments for the next few days."

"You're returning?" Thomas wasn't sure he'd heard correctly.

"Of course. You can probably expect half the cabinet to arrive throughout the week. Everyone likes to share in good news stories."

"Right. Mind telling me what the good news story is?"

Terence barked out a laugh. "Didn't Sara tell you? She and Jay discovered dinosaur eggs. Jay says he's never seen this kind before. One of them even has an embryonic femur sticking out... You still there, Thomas?"

"Uh...yeah, I'm here." Thomas couldn't hide his shock.

"Where is Sara anyway? She should have been here by now. I thought you'd take better care of that injury."

"What injury?" Thomas gripped the phone so hard his knuckles turned white. "She said she was fine."

"She gashed her left hand pretty deeply when she fell down that slope. You'd better get her in here for stitches."

"I'm on it."

Thomas hung up. He leaned back in his chair, still stunned.

"What is it?" said Patrick.

"You are not going to believe it. We have to find Sara."

He headed out the door at a run, Patrick keeping pace beside him.

At Sara's tent Thomas nearly tripped over Barney, who was lying across the entrance. He pulled Barney away and Patrick unzipped the flaps. He shook his head.

"She's not there?" Thomas stuck his head in to look for himself.

"Apparently not. Mind telling me what's going on?"

Thomas filled him in. Patrick shook his head, looking every bit as stunned as Thomas still felt.

"Get Sam to check the women's bathroom," Thomas said. "I'll go see if Dave knows where she is."

Dave, with Laura's help, was busy practising a scene from *The Importance of being Earnest*. "Sara's not here," he informed Thomas coldly. "I saw her walking up the road with her bag."

Love in the Age of Dinosaurs

Thomas felt the bottom drop out of his world. "You saw her leave? Why didn't you stop her?"

Dave glowered. "There wasn't anything I could possibly do or say to stop her. I wasn't the one who drove her away."

Thomas raced back to the field office, arriving at the same time as Patrick, who reported that no one had seen Sara. The message light on his phone was flashing.

With a trembling finger, he pushed the play button.

"Hey, Tom, I dropped Sara at the hospital in Brooks. Don't know what you folks meant, lettin' her hike away when she's hurt."

chapter

TWENTY-SEVEN

Sara dropped her bag on the floor and collapsed onto the bed. She closed her eyes briefly. *Just five minutes. Then I'll call Mary.*

She awoke around nine-thirty the next morning. She took her time bathing, partly because she needed the comforting warmth and partly because she was not supposed to get the sutures wet. She wore a plastic bag over her hand, but she did not immerse it in the bath water. It took a lot longer than usual to do everything with just one hand. After dressing awkwardly, she left the hotel room to get some breakfast. Then she checked out and called Mary.

"Where have you been?" Mary demanded when Sara entered her hospital room. "Any number of people are looking for you, and Patrick says that when he gets hold of you, he's going to shake you 'til your bones rattle."

"Why are they looking for me?"

"Oh, maybe because you disappeared without a trace yesterday. Did it ever occur to you that people might be concerned about your welfare?"

"No, actually, it didn't," Sara admitted.

"Well, why didn't it? Honestly, Sara, sometimes…"

"Because I've earned the contempt and dislike of everyone on the team, especially Thomas." She burst into tears.

Mary let her cry for a while before she started the third degree. Half an hour later, Sara had confessed all.

"So after I was released from the hospital, I caught the last bus to Calgary. I wanted to call you last night, but I fell asleep. I didn't wake up until this morning. I called you as soon as I could."

"I think you should call the camp," Mary said.

"No."

"They're all very worried about you. Especially Thomas. Patrick said he was fit to be tied when he found out you were injured. After Ben called and let them know he'd picked you up, they raced into Brooks, but you were already gone. Patrick called everyone we know to see if anyone had heard from you."

Sara sniffed miserably. "Is Patrick in the city?"

"He's at home. He should be back within the hour. And I have to warn you, Sara, he's really concerned."

"Meaning that if he sees me sitting here hale and hearty, he's going to feel such relief that he's bound to kill me," Sara guessed.

"Something like that."

"Okay, I guess I'll be on my way." Sara stood up to go.

"You can't leave," Mary said. "You need to let people know you're safe. I think you should go back to the camp and say goodbye properly to all of your friends."

Sara stared at Mary.

"They are your friends," Mary insisted. "That's why they're so concerned. Every single team member has called either Patrick or me to see if you've turned up. You need to respond to that outpouring of affection and concern."

"According to Thomas, I've undermined the team and ruined everything they were working towards. They're probably planning a public lynching."

"Thomas didn't mean it. He was exhausted, anxious, angry. We all say things we don't mean when we're in that kind of a state. He didn't mean it."

"He meant it." Sara couldn't hide her regret. "I wish I'd never gone to Dinosaur Provincial Park. I wish we'd never met. Then I wouldn't have fallen for him. I wouldn't have tried to help him, and I wouldn't have ended up ruining everything and earning his contempt. I'd rather not have met him in the first place than have him hate me."

Mary seemed to weigh her words before answering. "In the first place, Sara, you didn't ruin anything. The announcement of the find was made public this morning. The government wants to annex the area for the park. The funding committee doesn't give a rip who actually filled in the forms. And as for Thomas, it's not contempt he feels. From the moment he met you, he's been infatuated. Right from the beginning, he pumped Patrick about you. He's in love with you. That's why he gets so angry when you take chances or when he feels that you're endangered in any way.

"Before you came on the scene, I never knew Thomas to get angry with anyone but Dave."

Sara shook her head tiredly. "Well, whatever he felt before is gone now. It's the story of my life. I have such a tremendous gift for losing my nearest and dearest. I'll see you before I leave Alberta permanently." She gave Mary a hard hug. "Tell Patrick I'm sorry. I'll call him later."

She paused in the doorway and looked back. "Would you mind not telling Patrick where I'll be? Please?"

Mary regarded her for a long moment. "Only today, though. You'd better call Patrick yourself very soon. I'll call the camp and tell everyone that you turned up safe and sound and that you appreciate their concern. But Sara, you have to call Thomas."

Sara waved and left. She had one more place to go before she left the province for good. She could be there in three hours in a rented car.

Twenty minutes later, Thomas and Patrick walked in and found Mary on the phone.

"Yes, that's right, Dave, she just left here...No. I don't know where she's going, but she said to tell everyone there that she's fine...No, I—"

Thomas snatched the phone from her hand. "Dave, get back to work. I'll handle this." He hung up.

"Sara was here?" he said to Mary. "And you let her go?"

"Well, what could I do?" Mary said in a reasonable tone. "I'm hardly in a position to tackle her and tie her down."

Love in the Age of Dinosaurs

"No, but if you'd called me, I could have done it," Patrick said.

"Where did she go, Mary?"

Mary met his eyes and then looked away. "She didn't say where she was going, Tom."

"But you have an idea," he persisted.

Mary shook her head. "She promised to call. I can ask her then."

Thomas and Patrick exchanged a look over Mary's head. Patrick shook his head slightly.

"Okay, Mary." He sat beside the bed and took her hand. "I believe you know where she is, but you don't feel you can tell me. So I'm not going to press you further."

Mary exhaled slowly.

"For the time being. I'll give you and Sara three days. Then I'm coming back and you are going to tell me where she is. Are we clear?"

Mary nodded, her eyes huge in her pale face. Then she leaned back against the pillows and closed her eyes.

chapter

TWENTY-EIGHT

Sara stood barefoot on the sand, cotton pants rolled up to her knees, watching the sun sink behind the lowest cloud on the horizon. The last rays of sunlight sent golden streaks across the black water. She smiled sadly and reflected that life was always filled with endings.

But the knowledge that the sun will set need not shackle us to shadows or smother all our joy at sunrise.

Sorcha Lang

A feeling of peace washed over her and she picked up her sandals and walked back up the beach to the cabin. At the top of the steps to the deck, she stopped and stared at the wind spinner that was slowly rotating in the slight breeze.

"It seemed like a good place to hang it. I know you didn't mean to leave it behind."

Sara whirled to her left.

Thomas was sitting on the porch swing, looking relaxed and completely at home. A glass of ginger ale and a newspaper were on the low table in front of him.

A rushing noise filled her ears and she placed a steadying hand on the cabin wall as the world tilted at an alarming angle. She stood paralysed and speechless. Just as suddenly, her vision cleared, the numbness receded. With the tingling return of sensation, she found her voice. "On the contrary, Dr. McBride. I did mean to leave it behind. Just as I mean to leave you behind. Again."

She stalked to the cottage door and, once inside, locked it behind her. For a few seconds, she leaned against it, her heart pounding. How utterly appalling that she should be so happy to see him.

She started towards the fireplace, but stopped mid-stride as she caught sight of the expertly laid fire that had replaced the ashes from the night before. A sizable stack of wood was beside the fireplace, ready to be added when the fire was going well. All that remained was to open the damper and light a match to the newspaper. In front of the fireplace, the table, covered in a white damask cloth, had been set for two. A lovely crystal vase was filled with a beautiful bouquet of blue and white forget-me-nots, red geraniums, and purple hyacinths, all flowers that in another lifetime had once glorified her mother's garden.

Love in the Age of Dinosaurs

With a pang, Sara heard her mother's voice. *Forget-me-nots for hope and love, geraniums to proclaim your love, and purple hyacinth to ask forgiveness.* As she stood there, Thomas unlocked the front door and came to stand beside her.

"Dinner in five minutes," he announced. He lit two candles on the table, and they filled the otherwise dim room with a warm glow. He disappeared into the kitchen.

Feeling dazed, Sara walked down the hall to the bathroom. When she looked in the mirror, her green eyes were enormous in her pale face. After drying her hands, she walked slowly back to the living room and sat at the table.

"Cheese fondue." Thomas set plates of chopped vegetables and French bread on the table. "And chocolate fruit fondue for dessert."

Sara stared at the bubbling cheese in the fondue pot. "How long have you been here? And why did Patrick give you those keys?"

"Two hours, and because I asked nicely." Thomas handed her a flute of champagne. "Cheers." He touched his glass to hers.

Sara said, "I have no idea why you're here, but I can assure you that you will be leaving as soon as we have eaten."

"I came to tell you that you're fired."

"Hardly necessary." Sara returned his smile, but put no warmth in it. "I already got that message, loud and clear. Which should not be a surprise to anyone with your superior powers of observation. If I remember correctly, you were there to observe the occasion." She sipped her champagne. "Fortunately for me, I'm not dependent on you for my livelihood. I do have another job. So why don't we toast my return to the employ of Andrew Turner." She raised her glass in a mock toast and took a larger drink.

Thomas raised his glass in an answering salute. "Unfortunately for you, Andrew did the firing."

Sara set her glass down with a thunk.

"Careful. That's your mother's fine Waterford crystal."

"That is not funny, Thomas."

"I wasn't intending to be funny," Thomas said. "There is nothing funny about wanton destruction of your mother's fine Waterford crystal."

"That is not what I meant, stoopid." She threw her napkin on the table and stood, so suddenly that her chair tipped over.

"Sit Down. Right Now!"

The words cracked like a whip. Never having heard that tone of voice from Thomas before, she admitted to herself that he was a little scary. She stood her ground for a full three seconds, until he pushed back his chair and started to rise. She sat back down.

"I think we'd better replay the last part of that conversation," Thomas said pleasantly. "I will say again, 'There is nothing funny about wanton destruction of your mother's fine Waterford crystal.' Now it's your turn." He wore an expectant expression.

Sara said nothing.

He sighed and pushed back his chair again.

"That is not what I meant, you fool…" She added quickly, as Thomas got to his feet, "…around too much."

Thomas started around the table.

Sara hastily stood and started to back up. "What are you doing?"

"I really don't think you are capable of carrying on a civil conversation at the moment, so I am altering our plans for the evening."

Love in the Age of Dinosaurs

She decided that conversation was probably preferable to any other plan he might have. She backed up some more. "We can converse. I'll be civil."

"Too late." Thomas advanced on her. "I don't feel like conversing anymore."

"It's never too late to engage in the lost art of conversation." Feeling desperate now, she backed into the wall.

Thomas pounced. He trapped her against the wall, one hand on each side of her head. "Conversation with you is not a lost art; it's a lost cause. So we are going to abandon it."

He tucked a lock of hair behind her ear. "But because I understand how upsetting it must be to hear that Andrew has fired you, I'm going to give you a choice. You can persuade me as nicely as you know how not to express my dismay at your rudeness. Or you can live recklessly and let me demonstrate how dismayed I am at your rudeness. Choose carefully, Sara, because I warn you, I am very dismayed."

"You really are insufferable," Sara snapped. "You enter my cottage uninvited, use things that don't belong to you, threaten me. All because you're bigger and stronger and faster and more ruthless."

"Yes, that's all true. But I have to say that it doesn't really sound like you are trying to persuade me as nicely as you know how. I'm starting to think that I should just go ahead and show you how dismayed I am. Then perhaps we'll be able to sit comfortably and have a civil conversation. Or at least one of us will be able to sit comfortably."

Sara took a deep breath.

Thomas nodded knowingly. "A painful choice, I know. Why don't you let me assist you?" He bent and placed his lips on hers.

She tried to push him away.

"All you need to do," he said, his voice filled with gentle laughter, "is give me one nice kiss. Then we can go back to our dinner."

He kissed her again.

Sara's lips parted and for a split second moved with his before she clamped them tightly together and tried to avert her face.

He raised his head and looked her in the eyes. "Sara, this is your last warning."

"I gave you a kiss."

"No, you didn't," Thomas said. "*I* gave *you* a kiss. Not at all the same thing. And I know you know how to kiss me back. So let's replay the scene, Sara. Until we get it right, we're not moving on to the next act."

He bent his head again.

Sara closed her eyes and braced herself for his bruising kiss. Just get it over with. Keep it impersonal. Don't make a fool of yourself and don't, just don't, show him that you still love him.

He began.

She went very still. Resolve became uncertainty.

This was not as she'd expected.

Gentle kisses landed on her forehead, eyelids, nose.

His lips fluttered softly against hers. Light feathery kisses that asked for nothing in return softly landed and then took wing again.

For a long time, Sara received without responding.

Thomas's gentle fingers tilted her chin towards his own and then softly, so softly, caressed her face and neck while his lips touched hers and left and touched again.

Love in the Age of Dinosaurs

Her heartbeat slowed as his gentle stroking lulled her fears and smoothed all hurt away. She wanted it to never stop. She felt herself begin to drift, seduced by floating fingertips and even gentler lips. A faint warning rustled far away, but then died down. Almost imperceptibly, her own lips parted slightly and began a gentle pulsing.

Were they moving of their own accord? Or of her volition? It didn't matter. Nothing mattered but his touch.

So soft, so gentle.

For a long time, he demanded nothing more. She did not know when the change occurred, or who initiated it.

It might have been her.

His caresses steadied, became smoother, more drawn out. His lips, still light, tarried just a little longer with each brush against hers. And as Sara's own began to linger, each kiss melted into the next in a fluid and unending stream. To hesitate, to dam the flow would surely end existence.

Her needs became more urgent. Thomas deepened his kiss. She opened her mouth to receive his tongue and as his tip touched hers, the pleasant warmth that had suffused her body burst into roaring flames of desire.

Her nipples hardened. She arched her back and thrust herself against his hardness.

You're wanton. Don't do this.

The cold voice of reason intruded suddenly. It was too late. Sara thrust it savagely from her consciousness.

Thomas pulled her tight against him. As his fingers found her breasts, she gave a moan of pleasure and passionately kissed him back. She threaded her fingers through his hair and moved in rhythm to his stroking.

Thomas pressed her closer to the wall. He thrust his thigh between her legs. His forceful kisses, one after the other, each more desperate than the last, assaulted her lips and stole her breath away. His hands, so confident and sure, seemed everywhere at once, not seeking, but demanding her response.

She lost all sense of time, of place, of self-preservation. For this moment, for all time, nothing mattered but surrender.

The sudden, harsh jangling of a telephone jolted her back into awareness. She dropped her arms and stumbled back, appalled at what she'd done.

Thomas himself looked a little shaken, but he grinned at her wickedly. "I knew you could do it, Sara. You've almost persuaded me not to take offense at your earlier rudeness."

They returned to their dinner. Sara's lips felt swollen and her body was still on fire. She wished whole-heartedly that she hadn't responded so ardently to Thomas's touch. She burned with shame. She had practically torn the clothes off the man who had rejected her. She had thrust herself upon him and revealed not just her lust, but her love—which he didn't share. She had totally humiliated herself. Worst of all, if he gave her half a chance, she knew she'd do it all again.

Fat chance of keeping my love a secret if I respond like that every time he crooks his finger at me. I can't have Thomas, but at least I can have some self-respect.

"To unemployment." Thomas raised his glass.

"Here's to them that wish us well," Sara responded, as she raised hers, "and you yourself can go to he—"

Thomas raised an eyebrow.

Sara forced a smile. "Sorry. I think I must be a little drunk with pleasure."

"Eat your supper, and let's hope you sober up in a hurry."

Love in the Age of Dinosaurs

Sara smiled sweetly, speared a piece of bread, and dipped it into the melted cheese.

ೂ⊰

Sara closed the cupboard door with finality. An icy calm replaced her earlier passion. Thomas would never be hers. He had merely been playing with her emotions and had probably enjoyed humiliating her. Now she wanted him to leave. She would tell him so.

She paused in the doorway.

Thomas had moved the table against the living room wall. He had a fire burning and the music of Leonard Cohen floated across the room.

Thomas held out his hand, and asked softly, "May I have this dance, Sara?"

Sara was not accustomed to hearing that hesitant note in his voice. His uncertain smile tugged at her heartstrings. She felt the icy wall around her heart begin to crack. She held out her hand in acquiescence.

He turned it over to show the stitches, shook his head slightly, and raised it to his lips.

When he took her in his arms, Sara stiffened a little to maintain space between their bodies. At his raised eyebrow, she said, "If you have gotten me fired, you must know that you can hardly expect us to remain on speaking terms."

"You've always been much too modest about your own achievements." Thomas pulled her close and began to waltz her around the room. "Don't blame me if you made a marvellous discovery that was picked up by the press. Andrew read it in the papers and turned up on my doorstep spitting fire. And it's entirely your fault I want to keep you with me. You and you alone are responsible for that fact. I can hardly be blamed if the only way to get you was to get you fired. Sometimes you just have to do what you have to do. Isn't that what you told Dave?"

"You want to keep me with you?" Sara came to a standstill. She searched Thomas's face.

He nodded and resumed dancing.

"What as?" Sara pulled slightly away from him. "Chief cook and bottle washer?"

Thomas drew her closer again. "Chief cook? I didn't know you had ambitions in that area. Alas, the position has already been filled. Dave would probably be happy to have you back as an assistant, though."

Sara laughed as she shook her head.

"However, there are two other positions that need filling and you're a perfect fit for both."

"Hewer of wood or drawer of water?"

Thomas chuckled. "I'm thinking more along the lines of wife and colleague."

Sara stumbled, but Thomas didn't miss a beat.

"I love you, Sara, and I don't want to lose you," he said simply. "It's probably hard for you to believe that after the unforgiveable and untrue things I said. I've spent the last few days wondering how I could have been so cruel to the one I love the most. I can only hope that someday you'll believe me when I tell you how much I love you.

"I didn't know there was anything missing in my life until you came along, and now I can't imagine my life without you in it. I only hope that my presence in your life gives you the same joy."

Happiness warmed Sara's entire being as the glacier that had frozen her feelings suddenly melted away. She opened her mouth to reply.

"No, don't say anything right now." Thomas softly touched her lips. "You need to think it through. I'm asking a lot. I'm asking you to stay in Alberta with me, for us to make a life together. It will mean leaving your job with Andrew."

"I thought Andrew had fired me."

"I'm pretty sure I can get you reinstated, if that's what you really want."

He pulled her close and spoke softly into her ear. "I have to get back to the park. But in a week, I'll want an answer."

Sara closed her eyes and floated as the strains of "Dance Me to the End of Love" filled her being and she and Thomas moved as one.

chapter

TWENTY-NINE

A week later Sara stood with Barney at the site where the dinosaur eggs were being excavated. So far, the team had located nine separate nests in the area. The eggs were large and nearly spherical. Many contained embryos. Fossilised hatchlings had also been found. It was a spectacular discovery.

The press and the public could not get enough of it. Thomas's phone had been ringing off the hook since the original announcement, and he had extended the field season to facilitate the excavation.

It was getting close to sunset and most of the team had returned to the camp. Thomas finished covering the quarry he was working on and straightened. When he looked up and saw her, a beautiful smile lit his face.

He came toward her and she walked into his arms. "I could stay here forever," she said. When his arms tightened around her, she responded wholeheartedly, determined to let him know the depths of her feeling for him.

Behind her she heard Dave say, "So is this the result of loving dinosaurs?"

"It's the result of love," Patrick answered. "Love in the age of dinosaurs."

Their voices faded to a distant murmur when Thomas's kiss promised her a future as enduring as the fossils they would seek together.

ABOUT THE AUTHOR

Her friends claim that Sorcha Lang leads an unreal life. In reality, Sorcha enjoys a fortunate life filled with many diverse interests—music, travel, research, teaching, archaeology, palaeontology, sports, sewing, literature, linguistics, steam engines, classical dance. Greatly intrigued by the people she meets and the stories they tell, she collects both on her journeys. She is known to juggle many tasks simultaneously, but reports that she has been seen in several places at the same time are probably greatly exaggerated.

Made in the USA
Charleston, SC
28 October 2012